# Into

## Journey In Faith Series
## Book One

Beverly I. Sanders

ISBN: 9781703441024
ISBN-13: 978-1703441024

# DEDICATION

To the Congregation of McFarlin United
Methodist Church

*Into The Unknown, Book 1: Journey In Faith Series* is a work of fiction. Names, characters, places and incidents have historical reference but ultimately are products of the author's imagination or are used fictitiously.

# CHAPTERS

# ACKNOWLEDGMENTS

As one finishes a work such as this one, it is an absolute necessity to thank the people who have been instrumental along the way in making possible its completion.

At the beginning, which I believe was in 2017, there were the members of the 100th Anniversary Committee. I sent my first chapter to Kathy Mash, Pam Randorf, Linda Goodman, and Daphne Fix with the question whether the concept of telling the story this way would really work. They sent back encouragement to continue and have continued to encourage me at all steps along the way.

Then, there has been my patient husband, Joe Sanders. He put hundreds of miles on our van taking me all over central Oklahoma to museums, to the Conference Archives, and anyplace else I thought I might find a morsel of information. He has printed out pages and pages of information from the web to assist me in my research and my drawings. He has given suggestions for improving my story. When I began working on the drawings, he became my go-to source for critique. He has put up with months of the disruption of our lives as I have spent hours at the computer or the drawing board.

Daphne Fix was a great help as an early proofreader and she gave valuable suggestions to improve my format.

My daughter, Janice Mullan, gave hours of her time to read my manuscript for both content and correctness of grammar and spelling from the Language Arts teacher's viewpoint.

When we first visited the Oklahoma Territorial Museum in Guthrie, Oklahoma we were fortunate to meet Michael Williams, one of their directors. He spent a great deal of time discussing with me the different exhibits and the authentic glimpse they give of life on the Oklahoma frontier. In our conversations he shared a wealth of knowledge about everyday life on the frontier and invited me to contact him through email with additional questions. He has been faithful, prompt, and thorough with answers.

Finally, my son, John Sanders, has spent hours sharing with me what he has learned through his experience publishing his own works. We have spent many hours discussing how readers might react to certain writing styles and plots. Along with my husband, he has been a constructive critic of my attempts at illustrations, and has offered valuable suggestions for plot modifications. It is thanks to him that this book has been formatted and prepared for the printed version as well as the Kindle version. As a child, when he was having trouble learning to read, he was among the first children identified as dyslexic when it was just being discovered, defined, and treated! Who would ever have thought that he would become my primary guide in the writing and publishing of this book?

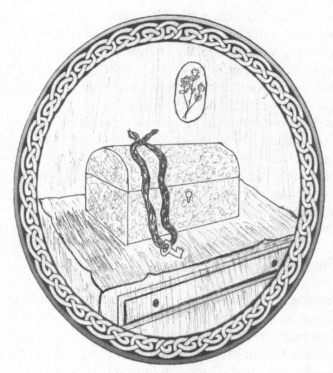

# Prologue

Melissa Conroy studied the little metal chest that sat on the nightstand in her bedroom. As she sat with a puzzled expression, she thought back over the events of the day that had led to this moment.

Today was her eighteenth birthday, May 20, 2022. The day had been celebrated quietly with her family. The party had included Melissa's parents, Janelle and George Conroy, along with her younger

sister, Marilyn, and brother Robert. They had
enjoyed Melissa's favorite dinner of baked ham and
scalloped potatoes, followed by a birthday cake and
presents from her family. Later, after all had gone to
their own rooms and the house was quiet, her mother
had come softly knocking on her door. When
Melissa opened it, Janelle stood there holding a
small beautifully embossed metal chest. It was
somewhat tarnished and worn, but still, it was
obvious it had been a beautiful treasure in its time.

As Melissa raised her eyebrows in curiosity,
her mother said, "I think it is time I gave you this
one more thing."

"Oh," said Melissa, "I thought we were all
finished with the presents."

"This is a different kind of present," said
Janelle, "You can accept this, or you may choose to
return it. After you have seen it and prayed about it,
you may let me know your decision. Unless you can
receive it with joy, you should return it, and there is
no shame in that. During the lifetime of this little
chest, there have been those who wisely rejected the
commission that comes with it. Take as long as you
wish to make your decision."

Janelle handed her surprised daughter the
chest and a small key attached to a faded piece of red
ribbon. She gave her daughter a quick hug and
moved away down the hallway.

"Wait," Melissa called, "I don't understand."

"You will," returned her mother, "Just look
inside."

Melissa closed her door, placed the chest

carefully on her nightstand, and studied it thoughtfully. It appeared to be about a foot and a half long, a little more than a foot wide, and about ten inches deep. Now as she was able to study the designs more carefully, she could see that it must once have been a beautiful silver color and that it was covered with embossed flowers and leaves twining gracefully around the top and sides. With age, the chest had taken on a lovely mellow patina, and it shone with a soft glow as the lights in her room were reflected.

She held the tiny key in her hand and hesitantly placed it in the lock. It turned easily and the lid creaked softly as she opened it. Inside were several small, books that appeared to be very old. Each was carefully covered with a clear plastic bag. She took out the one that appeared to be the oldest and opened it carefully. It felt stiff to her fingers, but she could see that the writing was still legible. A small piece of stationery, brittle and yellow with age, was tucked in front of the first page of the book. On it she read:

*If you are reading this message, you have been chosen for the job and privilege of recording God's care and guidance of this family. I received this journal and safekeeping chest in 1889 just before my family made the trip to The Unassigned Lands in a covered wagon to begin our new lives. I couldn't believe that my parents had given me such a wonderful, grown-up birthday gift. I knew that it was a gift meant to last a lifetime and that I must record faithfully my thoughts and stories, not just about myself, but of my whole family, our community and our church. It is also the story of how God has kept his hand on all of us and blessed us all as we have gone about the adventures of our daily lives.*

*Rebecca Simpson Cunningham*

Melissa turned the page and began to read.

*Hello, Dear Diary,*

*Wait! I can see already that that sounds funny. It seems kind of silly to be writing letters to a book! So, I think that I shall give you a name. I think that you will be Emmaline! I will write your name on the front of each book in my very best handwriting! You will be my best friend and share all the adventures of my life!*

*Hello, Dear Emmaline, (Doesn't that*

*sound better?)*

*My name is Rebecca Jane Simpson and we are going to be great friends!*

*This chest with its beautifully embossed designs is the most beautiful thing I have ever owned! Even the paper in the book is special. The wrappings on the book said, "The pages of this journal are made of the finest rag content paper to preserve your treasured thoughts for many years to come." Also in the chest were a beautiful fountain pen, a bottle of ink and a dropper to put the ink into the barrel of the pen. I had heard about these new pens, but never thought I would own one! My hands were shaking as I used the dropper to fill the pen and took it in hand to write on the fine paper of this special book!*

*I am 13 years old and was given this journal for my birthday just before we started our trip to the Indian Territory and the "Unassigned Lands." Both my birthday and this trip are like milestones in my life. At 13, I am no longer a child and I am starting the adventure of learning to be grown up. Mama and Papa say tomorrow will be another new*

*beginning, the start of a whole new
life! And now, I have this wonderful
new journal to record it all. It is so
beautiful I was hesitant to pick up my
pen. I must use my very best
handwriting and think carefully about
what to write before putting pen to
paper. But I worry too much. If I
don't start, this will remain just a
beautiful, but empty, book and that
would not be good, now would it?*

*We are here with our wagon
parked at a place called Downing's
Crossing along the South Canadian
River with what seems like thousands
of others. It is Sunday, April 21, 1889,
and tomorrow at noon, something is
supposed to happen; something that
has never happened before in our
country's history. All of these people
gathered here will get a signal and
everybody can rush into the
"Unassigned Lands." Everybody will
be trying to be the first to claim some
land for their own. It sounds very
exciting, but also maybe a little
frightening! We really need to do
some serious praying tonight! We are
so happy that we have found several
people who share our Christian
beliefs. Some say they are south
Methodists and some say they are*

*north Methodists. But from the way
we could worship and sing together, I
am not sure it makes much difference.
There is even one family of Baptists,
but they sing and pray just like we do!*

> *This morning a large group of
us got together to sing some hymns,
read the Bible, and pray together.
Mama and Papa talked with some of
the other families and they all agreed
that they would like to stake their
claims at a place called Norman
Station. So, this afternoon our wagon
and five others came north along the
river to a place called Downing's
Crossing. They believe that from here
it will be a much shorter drive to
Norman Station and they will have a
better chance to find a good claim.
Everyone seems so tense and excited.
There may not be many people
sleeping tonight. I feel sure that I
won't be able to close my eyes. I can
hardly wait...*

As Melissa read Rebecca's words, written so many years ago, it was as if the people and events she read about played out their stories on a huge screen in front of her eyes.

# Chapter 1

## Into a New Life

Easter Sunday, April 21, 1889, had dawned bright and crisp at the frontier town of Purcell, Indian Territory. Along the south bank of the South

Canadian River, wagons, tents, and open-air camps were crowded into every square inch of space. The fragrant smell of wood smoke was in the air from the hundreds of cooking fires being kindled at the camps. Soon, the aromas of cooking bacon and flapjacks began to fill the air as hopeful settlers rose from their bedrolls and prepared for a final day of waiting.

Many of those gathered there were faithful Christians, and they felt a desire for some special observation of the holiest of all Sundays: the celebration of the Lord's resurrection. As the sun began to climb above the eastern horizon, a clear musical sound rose from down near the riverfront where two wagons were drawn together beside a shared campfire. The words sung by a woman's clear voice fell sweetly into the morning quiet of the awakening campsites.

> *Holy, holy, holy! Lord God Almighty!*
> *Early in the morning, our song shall rise to*
thee.
> *Holy, holy, holy! Merciful and mighty,*
> *God in three persons, blessed Trinity!*

Soon people could be seen making their way through the hundreds of wagons toward the sweet sound, many joining their own voices in the familiar, well-loved words. By the time they reached the final, "... blessed Trinity," a large group had made their way to stand around the two wagons. As one song ended, someone would start another, and joy filled the air as more and more people joined the impromptu group. The more they sang, the more beautiful it became, and the more intricate the harmony.

The clear leading voice belonged to a young woman who stood in one of the two wagons with a hymnal in her hand as those gathered around joined in on their parts:

*Christ the Lord is ris'n today, Al - le - lu - ia!*

*Sons of men and angels say, Al - le - lu - ia!*

*Raise your joys and triumphs high, Al - le - lu - ia!*

*Sing ye heav'ns and earth reply, Al - le - lu - ia!*

With one final "Alleluia," all became quiet. A man stood up beside the woman in the front of the wagon. "My name is James Carpenter, and this is my wife, Charlotte," he said, "Out here as we are today, we all thought we wouldn't be able to celebrate Easter Sunday. Our God knew better. He has provided us with a more beautiful setting than we could imagine. We are blessed that He has brought us to this magnificent cathedral of land and sky. He has blessed my wife, Charlotte, with a beautiful voice to lead us in His praises. Maybe you feel, as I do, that it is time to join together in praying the prayer of Jesus."

And there in the serene quiet of the morning, many voices joined in as they prayed the timeless words:

> *Our Father who art in heaven,*
> *hallowed be thy name,*
> *Thy kingdom come, thy will be done,*
> *On earth, as it is in heaven.*
> *Give us this day our daily bread, and*
> *forgive us our trespasses,*
> *As we forgive those, who trespass*
> *against us.*
> *For thine is the kingdom and the*
> *power and the glory forever. Amen.*

In the quietness following the prayer, Mr. Carpenter continued, "I was reading the story of that first Easter morning from the book of John last night, and I was thinking, 'We may be setting out for a new life in a new territory tomorrow, but Jesus was preparing those early followers for a journey into a whole new kind of life that had never been heard of before.' Just listen to these verses." Those gathered around quietly listened as he read the timeless story of Jesus' appearances to his followers after His resurrection, and His instructions to them. One by one, the listeners began to offer comments on the reading and whether it had any relevance to their situation as they waited there until time to enter into the adventure of their own new lives in the Unassigned Lands.

"I can't say if the Lord has called us to settle this land," said a man with short brown hair and a neatly trimmed beard to match. "In fact, I know that this opening of the land will put a hardship on some of those Indian tribes who had lived on it before. I believe we are all God's children, and I wish our government had seen their way clear to find a way for us to share the land. But I do know that wherever we go, God has promised to go with us. My name is Samuel Groggins, and I have come here with my wife Miranda and our three children. We left everything we knew, sold our old farm and most of what little furniture we had. It is a scary feeling taking a chance with everything we have left in the world. I know that when we head into the new territory tomorrow, God will go with us, and whatever happens will be His will."

Others around the group nodded their heads in agreement, and another man stood up to speak, "Bridges is my name, Robert Bridges. Like you, I am certainly praying for God's blessing as we start out tomorrow. Those early Christians met a lot of opposition and how to deal with it was unknown to them. These 'Unassigned Lands' we are entering are not a complete unknown. The railroad men, the traders, and even the 'Boomers' have been in and out of this area for a good many years. They have talked about the area, and a few men have even decided just where they want to go and the best way to get there." Mr. Bridges waved a piece of paper above his head.

"I bought this newspaper, *The Arkansas City Daily News* before we left to come down here. It had this map in it. It may not be completely accurate, but I am going to bet on it. I have decided where I will be heading at noon tomorrow just as fast as I can get there."

There was an excited murmuring among those gathered there as they began turning to each other with surprised or doubtful faces. Soon after that, the impromptu gathering started to break up, and the eager settlers drifted toward their wagons.

Several of the men remained gathered around Mr. Bridges, and they began to question him about his plans for tomorrow. He smoothed his paper map on the tailgate of the wagon as the others moved closer to see.

"This right here," he said, "is the railroad track. I figure it is going to be important to us. If we are going to be farmers, we will need a way to ship our products. We also need to be near a town. I know my wife would not be very happy with a claim way out on the prairie, with no shopping, no neighbors, church, or school."

Those gathered around smiled and nodded at each other in agreement thinking about the needs of a family. As the conversation continued, some of the settlers left the group to follow the enticing aromas of lunches cooking back in their camps. Five of the men stayed on and on, becoming more and more excited as they studied Mr. Bridges' map.

A man who had been listening quietly and carefully introduced himself, "My name is Daniel

Simpson. I am here with my wife, Rachel, and daughter, Rebecca. We will be looking tomorrow for a farm that we can claim and live on for the rest of our lives, and our children's lives after us! So, we want to know as much as we can before we start. Time for making decisions will be short tomorrow after the signal. Can this map give us any help about where would be best to go?"

James Carpenter stepped up to the map, pointed to the railroad tracks and said, "I had some of the same thoughts and felt like I sure would like to know as much as I could find out about the land. So yesterday I spent a few dollars on a train ticket while we were waiting in Purcell and rode to the north border of the territory and then back again. I saw some mighty interesting things."

The others crowded in closer and began an excited murmuring. "Tell us what you saw," said Daniel Simpson. "What looks to you like the best place to head for?"

"Well," said James, "I plan to claim a town lot and set up a general store, so I was most interested in the railroad stops that are planned as town-sites. There were a lot of people on the train that seemed to have the same idea. There was a group that had been in and out of the territory lots of times. They called themselves Boomers. They had been working to convince the government that they had a right to claim these lands a long time ago. Claimed it was public land since it wasn't assigned to any of the Indians. Since they were so familiar with the countryside, I tried to listen to what they were saying," he continued, "They talked about Oklahoma Station having a lot of activity there already, and we just might be too late for the good lots. Guthrie is pretty far north; it would take quite a while getting there from here. But now this place here, Norman Station, it looks like it would be just what we need." He pointed to a spot on the map and the others crowded in close to see. "The Boomers seemed to think so, too. They tried to get off the train there, but the soldiers were there and wouldn't let them leave the train. They told them that they had to wait until tomorrow."

"Look here," said Daniel Simpson excitedly, "Here is Norman Station, and look just west of it. See these marks along the river. These are some places where there is known to be a safe crossing available. That's important because I hear that the river is just full of quicksand." Daniel was pointing to a spot a little farther north along the South Canadian River. "If traders and Indians and Boomers have been using these spots to ford the river safely, I can't see any reason why we can't cross there too, when it's time."

Robert Bridges took a closer look and scratched his chin as he mused, "Why, if a fellow could go in here at this crossing called Downing's, it couldn't be more than a three or four-mile run to Norman Station."

The others crowded around for a better look. "You know," said a man called Roger Harris, "I think it just might be worth a chance. I plan to get a town lot where I can start a livery stable. That just might give me a better chance to get a first-rate claim!"

"Maybe," said the man who had identified himself as Samuel Groggins, "but it just might be, too, that someone is trying to mislead a few people to a bad crossing and cut out some of the competition."

A young man with light brown hair and a neatly trimmed beard slipped in closer to the map to get a good look. "I sure like the looks of that," he said, "and since those Boomers seemed to think it would be a good place to go, I say it would be worth taking that chance, or my name's not Harvey Miller."

Daniel pointed to the map again, "See this area right here? I talked to a trader from Purcell, and he said to watch out for the area a few miles east of the railroad tracks around Norman Station. It is what they call the cross-timbers. Says that the trees and underbrush are so thick even dogs and cattle can't make their way through. If you are going there, be careful not to go too far east, because I don't think there will be time to go look things over and come back!" Mr. Simpson gave a little chuckle at his own attempt at humor.

The discussion went on and on until finally Mr. Robert Bridges, who had first produced the map under discussion, folded it and put it carefully in his pocket. "I, for one, am going to do it. I am going to move on north up the river today. I will be at Downing's Crossing tomorrow when the signal comes at noon."

"I will join you," said Mr. Simpson. "With the hundreds that are here, we would take an awfully long time just to get across the river. Maybe there won't be so many up there at Downing's."

One after another the other men standing around nodded their heads in agreement and moved back to their wagons. Six families had agreed to meet as soon as their lunches were finished and then travel together along the river bank to the place called Downing's Crossing.

"I sure hope there really is a ford there," said Roger Harris. "I guess if there is a problem, at least there will be six of us to work it out together.

**\*\*\*\***

The families finished a quick lunch and packed their belongings into their wagons. As soon as they had all gathered outside of the camp, they formed a small wagon train headed northwest on the trail with Robert Bridges in the lead. They followed closely along the river and soon came to a small gathering of wagons camped on the bank.

Robert stopped his team and called out to a few people lounging around, "Howdy, is this Downing's Crossing?"

A tall man near the campfire turned and acknowledged the group, "Howdy yourselves. Nah, this isn't Downing's Crossing. That's on up that way just a bit." He pointed northwest along the river. "Are you planning on crossing there?"

17

"That's what we're thinking. You crossing here?" continued Mr. Bridges.

"Yeah," said the tall man approaching the wagon, "There seems to be a pretty well-worn trail here going into the water, so we figure it must be a pretty good ford." By now several other people had come to gather around the speaker, curious about the newcomers.

"I think we will continue on a little farther up to Downing's." Mr. Bridges flicked the reins and started his team. "We wish you God's care and blessings tomorrow," he called as they pulled away. As they continued on their way, the people in the camp and those in the wagons called out goodbyes to them and exchanged good wishes for tomorrow.

A short distance later they arrived at another crossing and soon verified that it was Downing's. They found fewer wagons there than at Purcell, but still enough to create a problem when everyone would be trying to cross at the same time tomorrow.

The six families chose a site and made camp close together. After camp had been set up the sun was just beginning to move down the western sky, and the men decided to walk around and meet some of those gathered with them at this river crossing. While they were gone, the women prepared for a little leisure.

Rebecca took advantage of the chance to get better acquainted with the children. She took them on a short walk to gather small stones and small branches. Soon they had built a little town with homes and stores enough to furnish a place for all of these families and more to live.

The children tired quickly of the game, however, and Rebecca then smoothed another space in the dirt where she began to show Anna Mae Groggins how to write her alphabet. Soon she had Anna Mae calling out the name of the letter as soon as Rebecca started to draw it in the moist dirt.

By the time the men returned from their explorations, they found that, with Rebecca entertaining the children, the women had enjoyed some leisure and still had time to prepare supper which was slowly cooking in the embers of the fire. With time to spare, they were ready to hear the men's reports of their explorations.

"Well," said Daniel, "I talked to a lot of people, and it looks like most of the people here are a lot like my family! Feeling a need to start over and thinking this might be their chance to do it."

"I talked to another man just starting his married life like we are," said Harvey with a smile at his wife Marian. "They had come for most of the same reasons we did."

Samuel Groggins spoke thoughtfully, "Like anywhere you go there are some of those out for trouble. Did anyone else notice that group of about five or six rough-looking characters? Swaggering around through all the camps, knocking things over, walking right through the middle of other people's camps! They didn't seem to me to be your ordinary idea of homesteaders."

"I did see them," put in Robert Bridges, "Several of them had bottles they kept passing around their group. I couldn't see that they had anything with them but some pretty worn-out horses."

"I saw them too, and I don't think I would like to see any of them turning out to be my next-door neighbors!" said James Carpenter.

"There was one of them that didn't seem to fit with the others. I only saw them from a distance, but his clothes seemed to be a little cleaner than the others." added Samuel Groggins.

Roger Harris listened to the others and added his own thoughts, "It's a big country out there. Room for all kinds. Or at least room to stay away from those that turn out to be undesirable."

As dusk began to fall, the women went to bring out the food they had prepared.

"Better enjoy a hot meal now," said Rachel, "We don't know where we will be or what we will be doing at this time tomorrow!"

"We need to give thanks now for both the meal and the company and ask for guidance for tomorrow," said Jannetta Bridges softly.

Daniel stood up and took off his hat. He gave his heartfelt prayer echoing Janetta's thoughts. When he said "Amen," the group began to serve their plates with the delicious smelling food.

# Chapter 2

## Get Ready, Get Set!

The congenial group shared their supper and passed the time visiting as the darkness deepened during the long, tense evening. God was much on their minds as they wondered what the next day would hold for them. The conversation drifted to the churches they belonged to at their former homes, and how much they would miss them. The Simpsons, Carpenters, Groggins, and Bridges families revealed that they had been faithful members of the Methodist Episcopal Church, South. The Millers were Methodists of the Methodist Episcopal Church which was the north branch of the church, and the Harris Family were Southern Baptists.

"Well," Mr. Bridges remarked, "It really doesn't matter much right now what church we were. There's not going to be any churches of any kind in the territory to start with."

"That is probably true," said Mr. Miller, "I think that maybe we will need to do just like we did earlier today."

"Doesn't it say in the Bible, 'Where two or more are gathered together...?'" put in Mr. Harris.

"And I think it means it doesn't matter that some may be north or south Methodists, Baptists or whatever else may come," said Mr. Carpenter teasingly as he clapped Mr. Harris, the lone Baptist, on the shoulder.

So it had gone throughout the evening. The darkness deepened with the little group gathered in the light of their shared campfire. Overhead, the bright quarter moon and the seemingly endless star-filled sky filled them with awe, as the little group strengthened their new friendships. Finally, darkness fell, and some began to drift away to put the children to bed or to seek rest in their own beds in their wagons. Soon the whole camp was quiet as they dreamed of the land they hoped to find tomorrow.

****

When daylight came on Monday morning, April 22, many were already stirring in the camp there at Downing's Crossing.

Women stirred the embers of their campfires and added new fuel so they could cook a substantial breakfast to prepare their families for the day. The camp was now more extensive than when they had arrived yesterday. Several more settlers had arrived last evening as darkness fell. As the waking settlers began to climb down from their wagons or come out of their tents, many of the men wandered down to the riverside while waiting for their breakfast.

The muddy water was rippling along at a good clip. "Looks better than it did yesterday. That thunderstorm last night didn't seem to make it any worse," said one of them.

"I noticed yesterday down at Purcell that it was looking pretty dirty and seemed to be moving a mite fast for crossing," said James Carpenter with a questioning look at the man who had spoken.

"There were some spring storms last week in the territory," the man continued. "Everybody was a bit worried about whether wagons would be able to make it safely across. Some of the people in Purcell were even considering waiting until the train was gone and then trying to pull their wagons across the railroad bridge and swim the horses."

"Sounds kind of dangerous to me," said

Samuel Groggins taking another look at the reddish water, realizing he could not see the bottom. "Do you think we will be able to get across here?"

The man who had been speaking earlier had an air of experience about him that led the other men to listen to what he had to say. "A lot of us woke up when that thunderstorm came up during the night. I stood out here with a few more fellas watching the river. It's a lot calmer this morning than it was then. I guess the rain went on down the river and is more likely to cause trouble there than it is here. It looks pretty good and still has a few hours to go, so I am going to try it. If it looks like trouble, we can string a rope across to help keep the wagons from drifting away."

Women began to call their husbands and families that the food was ready, and they better hurry if they didn't want to eat it cold. With some doubtful glances at the water, the men drifted back to their camps.

The six families of friends joined together for a shared breakfast and prayers for a safe and successful beginning for their new lives in the Unassigned Lands. They found that their prayers for guidance and protection sounded much the same whether they came from north or south Methodists, Baptists or any other denomination.

During the morning, the wives prepared food for a cold lunch that could be eaten quickly before the noon send-off. The men and boys around the camp busied themselves carefully reloading their wagons. They were very careful to be sure that everything was securely fastened in place. Everyone knew that there would be no stopping to pick up treasures that might fly off as they sped along the way to Norman Station.

To those on the river bank going about their preparations for the big moment, one thing became noticeable, there did not seem to be any soldiers in the area as there had been at Purcell. They began to ask each other quietly, "With no soldiers here to fire the signal, how are we going to be sure to leave on time?" Others asked, "What's to keep us from going on early and get a little head-start?" Still, others asked, "What's to keep others from leaving early and cheating us out of our chance for some of the better claims just because we were honest and waited until the official time?"

Some drivers started to look about themselves nervously, and began to work their way down closer to the river bank.

"When people start to move some of us who don't have a time-piece won't know if it is really time, or just some cheaters going in early!" This comment came from the father of a family parked next to the group of friends.

Hearing that, Daniel reached into his pocket and pulled out a large pocket watch. Standing in the bed of his wagon he held it up, "We know that there is a lot of good land in there. It would seem foolish to get a good claim, and then lose it because someone could say we went in early! I think I have a solution for those of us who want to do this run honestly to the letter of the law, but still, don't want to lose one minute of good time. My watch was set right at the correct time yesterday when we left Purcell. So, for those who are thinking like I am, I will watch the time and shout it out as loud as I can when it is straight-up at 12:00 noon. We still have more than an hour left now, so why don't we all just relax and rest here in the middle of God's great creation!"

During that long hour's wait, some people moved in closer to Daniel's wagon where they would be sure to hear him shout. Others slipped on down to the water's edge. From time to time during the wait, a splash would be heard, and a wagon might be seen coming out of the water on the far side.

When they had everything in readiness, the six families of new friends gathered around for more conversation, and they began to share more of their backgrounds and what had brought them to this spot on this memorable day.

Daniel Simpson and Harvey Miller both came from farming backgrounds and looked forward to finding a claim of fertile land where they could get a crop planted in time to have a plentiful harvest by fall.

Daniel explained, "We came here from Missouri. Ever since Rachel and I were married in 1875, we've been living on my father's farm there helping him. There were seven more of my brothers and sisters getting close to being grown up, and I got to thinking it was about time I should step out on my own. We had been saving for a long time to accumulate the money to buy a farm in Missouri. Then when I heard about this land, free for the claiming, of course, it sounded too good to be true! I had to come to check it out. We figure now, that those savings will be enough to cover our filing fee and cover the costs to get the new farm started. So, Rachel and I just loaded up our wagon with Rebecca Jane and what belongings we had, brought our savings, and headed this way. When we got to the territory, we had to decide to go around it to the south or north. The trail to the south just seemed a little more traveled, and that's the way we went. So, there we were in Purcell just waiting when we met all of you."

As Samuel Groggins prepared to talk, another splash was heard down by the water. Samuel just shook his head, "It looks like they would realize that if they have their claim disputed, they would lose it if it became known that they had gone in early!" After another moment of musing, Samuel continued, "Yep, I'm a farmer too. Trouble is, my farm in west Arkansas didn't seem to grow much of anything but rocks! I wasn't making much of a living for a wife and three kids. Surprisingly, that rocky old farm sold and brought in a little bit of cash. So, this seemed like a chance we couldn't afford to miss." His wife, Miranda, sat beside him within the circle of the six wagons. She was holding their baby, Brewster, who was not yet a year old, while their other children played together, staying close to their parents as they had been told.

Anna Mae, who was six years old, was

playing in the damp dirt helping to amuse Mason who would be three years old in another month. She had built a little fence out of broken twigs, with a small building also made of twigs. "This is our new farm in the territory," she explained to Mason, "and this is our house that Papa will build." Mason picked up a small twig and bent it in the middle. He placed it inside Anna Mae's fence and said proudly, "Dog!"

James and Charlotte Carpenter had come from the Baltimore area in Maryland. James' father had owned a general store, and James had grown up helping in it. He explained, "When Charlotte and I got married just a year ago, I started to think about how I was going to support a family. Being the last of six, I didn't think there was going to be much future for us in the family business. So here we are! I plan on finding the main street in town and claiming the best lot I can find where I can set up my own store. I have loaded my wagon with boxes, barrels, and crates of goods that I figure are the things most new settlers are going to want to buy. You all come to see me when you need supplies." He looked around the circle with a smile.

Robert Bridges and his wife, Janetta, had with them their one-year-old daughter, Mary Annette. "I'm a little bit nervous about taking care of a baby in a territory where it will be some time before we will have a house, and there won't be any stores or doctors nearby," said Janetta, "But Robert reminded me of how our ancestors had arrived in America under much more primitive conditions. We think with God's help we can do it!" she nodded her head emphatically.

"I've never done much you could call farming, In New York state where we came from, I was a traveling trader. Not a good way to earn your living for a family man. It meant always being on the road, and not much of a living for all that. So, when we found out about this land, we decided I should have a try at farming." explained Robert. "Trouble is that I know nothing about farming! I've always been a quick learner, though, and I will just have to learn as I go along. My family is depending on it, so I pray that I can!" He reached over and gently cupped Mary Annette's curly little head in his hand.

Harvey Miller nodded his head in agreement. "I guess we are pretty much in the same situation. Marian and I were married just about a week before we headed this way. I was the youngest of nine kids, and we lived on a farm in Pennsylvania. Since I was the youngest of five boys and four girls, my dad had my four older brothers to help him on the farm, and I didn't do a lot of farm work growing up I guess the truth is that my sisters kind of spoiled me. My situation was kind of like yours, James. Although my dad had a lot of land, there wouldn't be much there for each of us if all nine of us planned to live on our share of it. So, Marian and I both think, being young like we are, we can look forward to a little adventure, coming to this place to make a life of our own."

Recognizing that he and Robert were both inexperienced for the farming life they were hoping to enter into, Harvey looked to Daniel for support and suggested, "Maybe if we stay close together, we can find our claims near each other, and that way we can work together to clear the land and get started. I know that I have a lot to learn from those of you who have more farming experience than I do."

Daniel nodded in agreement, "You might say that farming is in my blood, and it would make me proud to be able to share a little of the love I have for the land that God has given us."

The only family who hadn't shared their hopes and plans were the young couple, Roger and Flora Harris. Roger scratched his chin and put his arm around his young wife. "Guess it must be about my turn," he said. "Flora and I married just a month ago in Wichita, Kansas. I grew up helping my dad run a livery stable there, and I am hoping to claim a spot in town to run a stable here. You may have noticed that I am driving a team of four horses. It's not really that my wagon load is so heavy, but my dad gave me a few horses to help me get started on my own. So, I figured I could drive four, and if I get my claim OK, I will start renting out the four horses I have with me. After my claim is secure, I can go up to Kansas and bring the other horses down. We had talked to some Boomers up in Kansas, and they advised trying for claims in the south part of the territory, said that many of the Boomers who had already been in the territory so much were going to head for the Oklahoma Station area. Sounded like Oklahoma Station is likely to be overrun. We decided to take their advice and went all around the eastern borders of the area to get to Purcell, figuring that might be a good place to start from. We've put a lot into getting this far. I guess if we don't get a claim we'll just have to turn around and go back, although I sure don't want to."

His young wife, Flora, smiling, turned to him and took his arm, "We will get a claim, Roger. You know we will! Everything has come together so well. It must be God's plan for us."

"It sounds like we're all depending on God for our guidance today," said James, smiling at his new group of friends.

They passed the time discussing the types of homes they would build and the best crops to plant. Each of those who planned to farm had brought a small precious stock of seeds for starting their first crops and had agreed that, after the first year, they would save seeds to share for the next year.

"I'm just a little worried whether we can clear land and then get wheat, corn, and cotton planted in time for a crop this year," put in Daniel, "but we are sure going to work hard at it!"

By now the sun was climbing toward its peak high overhead. Daniel checked his watch and called out to those around them, "Thirty minutes to go. Go enjoy your lunch!" While the families ate their prepared cold lunches, Daniel took one more good look around and still saw no sign of any soldiers or officials. As the crowd began moving toward their wagons, he pulled out his watch, drew a deep breath and said to their friends, "Well, I volunteered myself for a job, I better pay attention and be sure I do it right!".

Roger called to all of them as they left the circle, "Remember, you aren't gaining anything by rushing out at the beginning. Horses can't gallop full out pulling a loaded wagon for more than a few miles without rest. All you would do is wear out your horses and be stuck before we get there. Just set a brisk pace right at the beginning and stay with it. You should be able to keep it up the whole way to Norman Station. If that map is right, it looks to be only a few miles. God go with you, and we will see you in Norman Station."

Excitement filled the air as the hundreds of settlers sat quietly in their wagons waiting for that perfect hour of noon. The splash of someone going in early came more and more often. Men reviewed their plans over and over as they all waited there on the riverbank through what seemed to be the most endless minutes of their lives. Was there any detail they could have missed? Were all the members of their families carefully instructed in their roles in the race for their new homes? Did the young ones know to keep inside the wagon and hang on? Were the pole and flag prepared and ready to stake the claim on their land?

Hopeful settlers waiting there on the riverbank were in every kind of conveyance: wagons, buggies, and even a bicycle or two. There were some on horseback and some had even come on foot. The sun inched its way higher in the sky and the minutes crept on as men took their places on their wagon seats and took their reins in hand.

Daniel watched the time carefully, until on the

dot of noon, he waved his hat in one hand, brought it down in an arc, and shouted, "Yeeee Haw! See you in The Unassigned Lands, and may God go with you!"

# Chapter 3

## A Race to Remember

*Hello, dear Emmaline,*
   *It's me, Rebecca Jane, and*

*here I am again. Oh! What a day it has been, and what stories I have to tell you!*

*As it was getting closer and closer to noon, we were all in our wagons and waiting. Since Downing's crossing was just a small ford, no soldiers had been sent there to see that no one went over early, and to give the starting signal when it was time. Since not many people had any kind of time-piece, my Papa volunteered to watch and shout it out when it was time. My breakfast and lunch both felt like a hard lump in my stomach, and I kept trying to breathe deeply to still my excitement! My china doll, Sally, appeared to be observing me from my bedroll. She was given to me three years ago. Since she is made of delicate china, I have never really played much with her. I just dressed her each day and placed her on my bed where I could appreciate her beauty. Today, I had dressed her in old play clothes just as I was wearing mine. Her smiling china face seemed to be watching me and telling me, not to worry, it would all be OK. I picked her up and brought her over to join me where we could look out the back of the wagon.*

*I said one more prayer to God and
said amen just as we all heard my
Papa shout out....*

As Daniel waved his hat and shouted,
precisely at noon, the people who had remained there
to wait for the noon entry time moved quickly to
begin crossing the river.

Rachel said wryly to Daniel, "Well, at least
we know it can be crossed safely since those that
cheated and went ahead early got across all right."

Daniel threw his head back and gave a loud
laugh, "That's one way to look at it."

The six wagons which had followed the river
north from Purcell yesterday were all in a group
about halfway through the crowd. Daniel Simpson
slowed his wagon briefly as he approached a young
man who was on foot carrying a pack on his back
and a pole over his shoulder. The white flag on the
end of the pole was waving lightly in the cool
breeze. Daniel called out cheerfully to the man,
"Need a little help across the river?" The young man
answered as he quickly climbed aboard, "That would
be a real blessing! My name is Charles Cunningham,
and I'm heading over around Norman Station. I
guess it would be a pretty long walk in wet boots."

Approaching the river, they were careful to
stay within the traveled path as they went through
the sand, into the water, and out the other side into
the Unassigned Lands. Cheers erupted as the first
wagons safely reached the other side.

As the first of the six friends' wagons got

safely across, the driver waited until the next two had crossed, being sure that there were always two other men to help if they had any trouble. Then they began to move on along the wagon trail to the east.

Charles Cunningham prepared to jump from the Simpsons' wagon as it came out of the water. Daniel placed his hand on the young man's shoulder and said, "Why don't you just stay put? The horses are fresh, and if our figuring is right, it shouldn't be far to Norman Station. With only three of us in my family, one more in the wagon shouldn't make much difference."

Soon all six wagons of the group were across and the teams were moving two abreast at a brisk pace toward what they hoped would be their future homes to the east near the Norman Station.

All around them, riders were galloping on horseback and passing them on both sides. Many of those going by were trying to goad them into going faster. Sometimes another wagon racing along with a laboring team of horses would pass the whole group, with the occupants laughing and yelling at them good-naturedly for being slow. The drivers and families in the six wagons smiled and waved cheerfully as they continued their comfortable pace. Before long they began to pass some who had already jumped from their horses to plant their stakes in the ground. They passed wagons with broken wheels or exhausted horses. Most of them had simply pulled off the trail and planted their stake where they were, waving at those who continued past them.

Strangely, they also saw several places that had the appearance of an established camp, with tents already in place. In one place they saw people come dashing out from a grove of trees as the first wagons began to reach them. They hurried around driving their stakes before turning to wave at the passing wagons.

After observing several of these, Rebecca crawled to the front of the wagon and shouted to her father, "How could they possibly be here already and so settled in? Even the people who crossed the river early this morning couldn't be that quick!"

Daniel just shook his head and said, "The rules said no one could come in before noon today, but as we observed for ourselves there just weren't enough soldiers to be all over the territory, and some people were sure to come in illegally. They may even have been here for several days and just staying hidden. I am sure there will still be plenty of good land left where we are going!"

As they continued on their way, Charles Cunningham managed to introduce himself more completely even though he had to shout to be heard above the rattle and noise of their wagon and all the others on the trail. The whooping of excited men and the pounding of hooves added to the chaos. Charles revealed that he was just seventeen years old and had come from West Virginia. When his father had died two years ago in a farming accident, he, along with his twin sisters and his mother, stayed on their farm. Much of the farm was hilly and covered with small rocks. It was not very profitable, especially with only one very young man to farm it. "Mom's health is not very good. Even if I had been able to bring her and the girls on this run, she wouldn't have been able to do it. I hear that the head of a household can establish a claim. Our family is just me, Mom, Jennifer, and Jean. The girls just had their fourteenth birthdays right before we sold the farm. Legally they are still minors. So, I guess that makes me head of a household. Seventeen doesn't sound very old when the age to claim a homestead is 21. Surely, as the head of a household, I will still be able to stake a claim. I just figure it was God's plan that I saw that land opening story in the newspaper. I think God must have meant for us to come to this place. That doesn't mean it has been easy, though. The old farm didn't bring much when we sold it. There wasn't enough money for a wagon, or a buggy, or anything to get us here. So, we went ahead and spent some of the money for the train tickets, and I left my family waiting in a boarding house up north in Arkansas City in Kansas until I get our claim and get it registered. We decided it was best to spend a little more of our money for my train ticket to come all the way down here to come in from the south. I thought maybe there wouldn't be as many people here as at the north side. We put our money away in a bank up in Kansas and rationed out a few dollars for me to bring to eat on and pay the filing fee. Mom and the girls will be careful and only use what they have to. I'm hoping that what we have left is enough to keep them there and then to pay for the train to bring them down. Mom is not well enough to work, but the girls might be able to wait tables in one of the restaurants there or something like that while they are waiting. We're just praying that Mom will be strong enough to ride the train when it's time."

"I'm mighty sorry your mother's not well. For a young fellow, it sounds like you have had a rough road to hoe! You've made some pretty wise decisions! If you want to stay with us all the way to Norman Station, maybe you can find a claim close to us and our three other friends that plan to farm. I know I would be proud to have such a fine God-fearing young man and his family as neighbors and I know the rest would be too." With that, it was settled, and they all looked eagerly ahead, straining to see through the dust stirred up by the frantic rush. All were watching excitedly for their first view of the railroad tracks and the survey markers where they would plant their stakes and establish their new homes. What did God have ahead for them in this beautiful, unknown place?

Soon they saw that some of the crowd started to slow down and they could see that the reason was the need to work their way carefully over the railroad tracks, being careful not to break a wheel or axle. At about the same time, the Carpenter and Harris families made a turn to the south and, with waves to their new friends, shouted, "God go with you! Come see us in Norman Station!"

The railroad tracks were strung across the grassy prairie, looking like two shining silver ribbons. As one of the four wagons approached the tracks, the men in the three remaining wagons jumped to the ground, prepared to put a shoulder to the wheel if needed to get across those tracks. As the driver encouraged his team, the men gave a good lift and shove, and in this way, the four wagons were soon all safely across.

Daniel began to look carefully at the land as they drove quickly over it. All around them were fields of waving grass with small twisted trees that appeared to be a variety of oak scattered liberally throughout. He paused and leaned over the side of the wagon. "I never saw the like!" he said. "The dirt underneath that grass is as red as a big ripe apple! Wonder if being red will make it grow good wheat and corn."

A little farther on he stopped his wagon near a survey marker and jumped out. He pulled up a handful or the grass and shook the dirt from it into his other palm. Looking around him at the waving grass one more time, then down at the ground, he made a quick decision and quickly drove his stake into that red dirt. Charles Cunningham also jumped out and placed his stake right in the adjoining claim.

Their friends in the other three wagons veered slightly to the north until they came to survey markers for additional claims. The wagons stopped a half-mile to the north, and the Miller, Bridges, and Groggins families quickly started driving their stakes into the red soil, soft from yesterday's rain. As the Simpsons and Charles watched, they saw another man approach Samuel Groggins. The man began to wave his arms excitedly, shouting and pointing off to the northeast. Samuel removed his hat and scratched his head as he listened to the angry man. He listened carefully, then spoke calmly to the still agitated man. The man became quiet, and it looked as if he replied to Samuel. The two walked over to the Groggins' wagon, and Samuel unhitched one of his horses. The man, no longer angry, jumped on the back of the horse, and galloped off to the northeast. Now it appeared that the friends had managed to stake five claims clustered together.

"Looks like there was a question over which one got there first," said Daniel, as he and Charles started walking across the prairie toward the other three wagons.

When the group met and Charles was introduced to the others, he spoke to Samuel Groggins, "Looks like you managed to settle that disagreement in a friendly way," said Charles, "I guess there's a lot of people might be willing to take a horse in trade for agreeing to look a little farther for their claim."

Just a short distance away their friends began to climb out of the wagons and look around them. Samuel Groggins helped his wife, Miranda, from the wagon with one-year-old Brewster in her arms. He caught six-year-old Anna Mae just as she was about to jump, then gently lifted Mason Earl, who was not quite three, to the ground. Janetta Bridges handed their baby, Mary Annette, to Robert and climbed carefully over the wheel herself. The young Millers, Marian and Harvey, both jumped to the ground eagerly. As the four families and Charles stood together surveying the scene around them, they were all wearing broad smiles and were hardly able to contain their excitement.

"It looks like we did it," said Harvey Miller. He addressed Samuel Groggins as he and Miranda approached. "That was quick thinking on your part, Samuel!"

"Well," Samuel scratched his chin as he spoke, "It was an honest misunderstanding. With these claims being a half-mile on a side, it's hard to know whether there might already be someone on the far side. I kind of figured that, in exchange for a good horse, he might be willing to try his luck farther on. I hated to lose the horse but didn't want an argument. I just hope there's not someone else we don't know about over there out of sight on some of these other claims." They all shaded their eyes looking off toward the far sides of their claims.

Robert Bridges spoke up, "Being neighbors here like we will be, we can all share horses when we start breaking ground. We can make sure you are able to clear and plow your land. It will go faster if we all work together, anyway."

Rachel Simpson looked around happily at the group standing there together, "It looks like we all managed to stake out something. Let's pray that this area turns out to be good growing soil." She pointed off to the eastern horizon, "Look over there! I think it is a good thing we stopped here. That looks like a bit of woods, probably what they were calling the cross-timbers."

All looked off to the east where Rachel was pointing. Daniel looked around noting the waving grass and the small twisted trees around them. "You are right, that this was a good place to stop. We will have a few small trees to cut and pull the stumps, but just look over there to the east. Can you see how the growth seems to be getting thicker the farther you go? I think that must be the cross-timbers for sure. The tales they tell of it say it is so thick that even a dog can't get through it. A claim there would take an awfully long-time cutting trees and brush and pulling stumps trying to get it cleared." He knelt and pulled up a handful of the long grass. Again he shook the red dirt from the roots into his other hand and showed it to his friends. "If the land grows this grass so well, surely it will grow oats, wheat, and corn. There is so much wonderful land here that there should be plenty for all of these people." He stood and gazed around again, removed his hat, and held it over his heart as the others stood quietly around him and bowed their heads, "God you have truly blessed us this day. Thank you, Lord, for bringing us safely to this place."

# Chapter 4

## Off to Guthrie!

*Oh! Emmaline!*
    *Yesterday was just so unbelievable! It was frightening, yet exciting too as we raced across the*

*prairie with other wagons and horses
passing us on both sides. I was
worried that we were being left
behind and would find all the good
land gone when we got to Norman
Station. God was with us
though, and there were good claims
right here waiting for us! Now Papa
must go to Guthrie and leave us here
alone! That is really frightening! We
will have the women and children
from the other three families to keep
us company, but this is such a strange
new place that I just can't help being
a little afraid! I guess I just want
Papa to hurry there so he can get
back soon. We started learning what
it will be like living here...*

"We're going to need to go to Guthrie to get all these claims filed. The sooner, the better," said Daniel, looking at his friends and new neighbors. "Maybe we can all go together, and our wives and families can keep each other company here while we are gone."

The others nodded in agreement, and Harvey Miller said, "I guess we better get back to our places and do something to show that they are taken. We don't want someone else to come along and try to claim them while we are gone."

With this, they all headed back to their own wagons. The Simpsons and Charles Cunningham took a long look around. As far as they could see, there was waving grass seeming to make the land come alive with a wavelike motion. Many of the small twisted trees dotted the landscape along with several other varieties. Here and there a blooming plant could be seen mixed in the grass. The fresh breeze brought a faint, unmistakable scent of growing things.

Rachel Simpson put an arm around her 13-year-old daughter, Rebecca, and exclaimed, "What a wonderful place this is. We are really going to like it here!"

"This looks like a good choice of a place for our family," said Daniel Simpson. "It's a beautiful land, and we know our surrounding neighbors are going to be wonderful godly people," he continued, as he waved off to the north where their other friends had gone.

Charles turned to Daniel with a smile of appreciation, "I couldn't possibly have gotten here to claim this spot without your help. It's going to be a real blessing for me and my mom and sisters. I wish I could let them know right away how well things have gone!"

"We need to set up our camp as quickly as possible and then get on our way to Guthrie to get the claim filed. The rules say we have to start to make some improvements to secure our claim. I understand some people are figuring that, for now, a tent will count as an improvement. Maybe we should move on north a little, close to where the claims all come together and set up our tents there. That way,

the women can be close together while we are gone."
They climbed back in the wagon, and Daniel drove a
little farther north before stopping and saying, "I
figure this ought to do."

Daniel began to unload the wagon, and
Charles pitched in to help. With the efficiency
Daniel had learned from many days of practice on
their trip to The Unassigned Lands, they soon had
the tent, a table, chairs, and a few other items set up.
Charles was a quick learner and seemed to
understand just what he needed to do to help the
most.

Daniel looked around again with a thoughtful
expression, "Charles, I think we need to do
something on your claim, so it will be obvious that it
is taken. We can build a sort of shelter using blocks
of this prairie grass. If we can just put up one wall
for right now, we could use the extra canvas I
brought and make a sort of lean-to. That should
make it pretty clear that your claim is taken," he
said.

Charles nodded in agreement, and the two set
to work together. They chose a spot a few yards
away from the borders of their land and began to cut
large rectangular chunks of sod. They were careful to
be sure that the roots were left in each piece to
strengthen it and hold it together. They carried them
back to the spot on Charles' land where they had
decided to place his shelter. The chunks were
stacked brick style, and soon a low wall began to
take shape.

"This sure makes me thankful for that rain

yesterday," said Charles as he attacked the prairie grass with his shovel to cut another sod brick. "This is not so easy now, but it would be next to impossible if the ground was dry!"

Daniel agreed, and they continued at their task. After a few hours of hard work, the makeshift shelter was finished. The two men surveyed their work with a satisfied look.

By now the sun was moving toward the west, and Daniel looked around their little camp and then to the north. "I think we should go back over to my wagon about now. I just bet that Rachel has something good for us to eat."

They walked through the waving prairie grass back to the wagon where Rachel and Rebecca Jane were working around a campfire they had built. Rachel was stirring a huge iron skillet from which came sizzling sounds and delicious aromas.

Daniel took off his hat, grinning at Charles and said, "What did I tell you?" He looked around, scratched his head and continued as he looked over toward their friends' wagons, "I guess maybe we could catch the train to Guthrie in the morning, to get these places registered. The sooner, the better. It looks like our neighbors may be about ready to go too."

Rachel was not quick enough to stop the stricken look that crossed her face as she quickly put down the skillet and turned away. Daniel gathered Rachel and Rebecca Jane both in his arms and said, "I wish there were some way to register this claim without leaving you two here alone. Even though all the people we've met have seemed to be wonderful people, we know there are some out there who might try to take advantage of the situation and try to steal the claim."

"Nonsense," said Rachel with a shaky smile, "You won't be gone long, and we are perfectly able to take care of things. The four of us wives and the children will be camping right here together. You just get on your way first thing tomorrow morning so you can be back soon."

All the families had planned their budgets with enough money to pay for registering their claims and still have enough to catch the train to Guthrie where the land office was located. Charles expressed the feelings of all of them when he said, "I figure that about the most important thing I can do is to get to Guthrie as soon as possible and get this claim all legal!"

"If the five of us all go into town in one wagon, the women will have the other wagons and horses here if they need them," said Daniel as he and Charles made their way through the waving grass to the campsites of their friends to talk with the other men.

The men had made their plans to leave early the next morning and go into the new settlement at Norman Station. If their friend Roger Harris had claimed lots as he had planned, they could leave the horses and wagon with Roger in his livery stable while they caught the train to Guthrie.

The next morning everyone was up early, the women preparing a good breakfast before the men

were on their way.  They had decided to take Harvey
Miller's wagon and team, so after they had all said
their "goodbyes" to their families, they climbed into
the wagon and headed off into the new settlement of
Norman. Rachel Simpson with her daughter Rebecca
Jane, Jannetta Bridges, Marian Miller, and Miranda
Groggins stood together with their children gathered
around them as they watched the men go. In spite of
the bravado they had all shown discussing the
matter, their faces now showed varying degrees of
fear, worry, and sadness, and a wayward tear found
its way down more than one cheek. No one knew
how long the men would be gone. They had no idea
what they might find when they arrived in Guthrie.
The five stood arm in arm watching the wagon
disappear in the distance.

"Lord," said Jannetta, "please keep my
Robert safe and bring him back home."

"And my Harvey," said Marian.

"And my Samuel," said Miranda.

"And my Daniel," said Rachel.

"And my father and our friend Charles," said
Rebecca Jane.

They all exchanged looks with each other,
nodded and bowed their heads, "Lord we trust them
in your hands. You have brought us this far, and we
know we can depend on you, Amen," finished
Rachel.

With that, the women straightened their
shoulders, drew a deep breath, and put resolute
expressions on their faces.

"Let's all gather a few supplies and get

together up here where we share a common border. We will have an adventure, just us girls and the children!" said Jannetta.

They all turned back to their claims with heads held high and a determination in their steps, just as pioneer women had always done. They were confident they could handle this with God's help.

# Chapter 5

## Settling In

*Dear Emmaline,*
       *As I write this tonight, I can*
*admit to you, what I haven't wanted*
*to let anyone else see today as we*

*have worked with our new friends and
neighbors to start making our new
homes. It was so scary when Father
left with the other men to go catch the
train and get our new land registered.
Here we were! Mother and I and
three other women with their little
children and babies stood there
watching the men drive away. I am
the oldest of the children, so I felt like
I should not let them see how afraid I
was. We all stood around for a little
while after the men drove off headed
to the station to catch the train. Little
Anna Mae Groggins is six years old,
and her two brothers Mason and
Brewster are three and one. Mason is
a rowdy little guy, and Brewster is
toddling right behind him every step.
Little Mary Annette Bridges is just
barely one year old and not yet
walking. Anna Mae patted her
mother's face and told her not to cry.
I told Anna Mae to bring her little
brothers and then I took Mary
Annette from her mother...*

Rebecca Jane took all the younger children
over to a spot in the shade of their wagon where
Daniel had cleared some of the tall grass away. She
found a stick and drew a series of crossing lines on
the ground.

"This is called hopscotch," she told them as she demonstrated, "You have to hop through all the squares without touching any lines."

In no time Anna Mae and Mason were hopping along behind Rebecca Jane while Mary Annette crawled around through their feet. They laughed and laughed as little Brewster tried to hop on both feet, doing his best imitation of Mason. Soon they were rolling on the ground with laughter. So, the moment had passed; their mothers had all collected themselves and dried their tears. The women and their children headed back to their own wagons to clean up from breakfast and put the campsites in order. Soon there would be lunch to cook, and in the meantime, they would begin bringing a few of the treasures from their wagons to place in their tents. They would spend the time making this place look like a home for their returning husbands, tomorrow or the next day, or whenever they would return. All the while they kept busy, their earnest prayers were going quietly up, "Dear God, please bring them safely back and please make it soon!"

When the sun was high overhead, each of the women gathered her lunch supplies and went to join the other families. With much visiting and sharing of stories and dreams, the lunch was soon prepared and eaten.

"I am running out of a lot of my cooking supplies," said Miranda Groggins. "I wonder if we might be able to hitch up my wagon and go see if there is anything available in town."

"Well, the Carpenters had their wagon loaded with supplies to start their general store," Rachel said thoughtfully. "If we can find where they have located their store, they might have the things we need."

"Besides," said Janetta Bridges, "it will help the time pass!"

All the women agreed to gather again that evening for their meal. During the long afternoon, Rachel and Rebecca showed the rest of the women how Daniel and Charles had cut blocks of the sod to build Charles' shelter. The women all worked busily through the day cutting blocks to be stacked to make temporary shelters on each claim. It was hard, heavy work, and they soon found perspiration running down their faces and dripping off their chins. Brushing it away only resulted in dirty smears on their faces and clothes. They moved from claim to claim working together and carefully stacking like numbers of blocks at each campsite. Finally, as the sun was about halfway to the horizon, they straightened their backs and looked around.

"Oh my," said Marian Miller giggling and pointing at the other women, "Do we all look like that?"

"Even the babies," said Miranda Groggins snatching up her little one. "Just look at Mason and Brewster."

As they looked at each other, these hardy women giggled and then roared with laughter. Soon, for the second time during that endless day there were tears running down their cheeks, but they were from merriment this time.

"Let's all get cleaned up, and have a potluck picnic supper," said Rachel. "I have a pot of ham and beans already cooked."

"I have bread left that I made last night," offered Miranda.

"We have had a hard afternoon of work. We have certainly earned our supper!" said Marian, "I have some dried apple cobbler left."

With more fellowship to look forward to, the women left to get their contributions and clean up themselves and their children.

As they relaxed around their small campfire after eating their hearty meal, Janetta Bridges looked thoughtfully up at the sky. "I wonder if this sky looks as big and wonderful in Guthrie as it does here," she mused. "Just look at that big fat moon and those millions of stars."

"I am sure it does," put in petite Marian "I just know that Harvey is up there in Guthrie right now looking at these same stars and missing me just as I am him."

The other women looked at their young newlywed friend with understanding, motherly smiles. "I think they are all missing us and just wishing they were back here," said Rachel as she studied the vast sky. "It just didn't seem this big back in Missouri."

"They all know that this is hard for us, and I have a feeling that they are probably praying for us right now," ventured Janetta Bridges. "I know God is watching over all of us, and He will bring them back to us safely."

"Well," said Rachel rousing herself, "It is a good thing we put in a hard day's work. I, at least, am sure that I will sleep soundly!"

As the darkness fell, the women gathered their things and their children to go back to their wagons. They had agreed to hitch up the Groggins' wagon and find their way into town early tomorrow. That plan was enough to raise their spirits even facing the prospect of another long day without their men.

The four women and their children slept soundly through the night, waking refreshed and optimistic on Wednesday morning. Quick breakfasts were prepared at their campsites, and they hurried to help Miranda with the unfamiliar task of harnessing her team to the wagon. The horses seemed to know that something was not the same. As the women worked trying to remember how the men had done the harnessing, the horses were nervous, snorting and swinging their heads up and down, then side to side. Finally, after some frightening moments, the job was done and the horses calmed down just as if Samuel himself had been there.

Miranda put one hand on her hip and stood shaking her finger in the horses' long faces. "Now that it's done you decide to cooperate!" she said with a little quiver in her voice, "Now you act just like gentle little lambs!" She threw her hands up in exasperation and called out to her friends, "Well, everybody in!" She climbed into the driver's seat and took up the reins as the others climbed in and took their places. "Good thing I am better at driving than I am at harnessing. I often spelled Samuel with the driving on the way here."

Soon the wagonload of laughing, chattering women and children was on the way to a new adventure. They were eager to see these new places that were to become an important part of their futures. Ahead of them was the whole newly settled town of Norman waiting for them to explore it.

Miranda guided the team along beside the railroad tracks where the grass had already been beaten down, marking the way into Norman. It seemed that a lot of people had already been finding their way into the new town. It took them about thirty minutes before they came into an area bustling with activity and with tents thickly dotting the landscape. Many of the tents had hand-lettered signs attached to them advertising the services that the owner planned to offer there. The group of women and children drove slowly up and down the rows of tents reading all the signs. There were tents selling legal services and restaurant tents with good smells coming from the foods being prepared for lunch. There were stacks of lumber waiting for purchase by some of the many settlers eager to begin putting their new homes together. One especially large tent had stacks of feed for animals and nearby was a blacksmith selling and repairing wagons and wheels while several horses were waiting to be shod.

Before long they had found not just one, but several general stores. It took them some time, but they were finally able to locate their friends, the

Carpenters. Charlotte Carpenter eagerly greeted her friends with a hug and began to show them around the goods displayed in their large tent. Each of the four women replenished the supplies that had been used up on the trip to the territory. The children, made somewhat timid by the strangeness of the situation, stayed close to their mothers during their shopping. As they were settling their bills, Charlotte held out a huge jar of peppermint sticks allowing each child to pick one. The mothers took the treats for the babies saying that they would let them have some tiny bites later. The group stayed there while the women visited and the children became bold enough to venture up and down the aisles of the store while they contentedly sucked on their candy.

While they were still visiting, James Carpenter entered the tent and enthusiastically greeted the women and their children. In answer to their questions about why he was not in Guthrie, he explained, "When we got here, we found out that our arrangements for a city lot were to be made with the townsite company who surveyed the area and marked off the lots. So, I don't have to make the trip."

"He saw Roger Harris yesterday. They had found a nice place over there north and just a little way west of the tracks where he will have room to keep the horses for his livery stable." Charlotte put in. "The land company has set up in a tent just down the block so James and Roger were able to get our places claimed all right and proper."

The women continued their visit while James

loaded their supplies into the wagon. "Oh! I do have some news," said Charlotte, "We are hearing from some of our neighbors who happen to be South Methodists that there were both north and south ministers who came in on Monday and claimed lots for their churches to build on. There will be a prayer meeting on Sunday on the lots claimed by Mr. Charles Streeter whose claim is on the same block as the lots for the south church. I hear there will be lots of singing, praying and Bible study."

"That's good news," said Rachel, "That is something to look forward to.

After making sure they knew the location and time for the gathering, the women and children climbed into the wagon and drove away with promises to see them on Sunday. They drove out to the northwest where Charlotte had indicated the Harrises were settled. They were eager to say hello to Roger and his wife, Flora. They found the right place quickly with no problems, and they all climbed down from the wagon as Roger and Flora hurried to greet them. They soon found out that their husbands had also easily found the place when they had arrived on Tuesday, and that they had left their horses and wagon at the new livery stable to be cared for as planned. Roger had quickly removed the harnesses and pastured their horses then hurried to harness his own team to drive the men back to the station just in time to catch the northbound train.

The women concluded their visit, got into the wagon, and began their return journey to their new homes. As they were approaching the tracks, the air was blasted by the sound of a train whistle as it came south down the tracks and screeched to a halt at the small building that was in use as a depot. Miranda struggled with her horses who put their ears back and reared up, fighting against the harness. By her persistence, she was able to control them as the women watched a few people beginning to get off the train. Knowing that it was too soon, they still couldn't help thinking how wonderful it would be if their husbands might have finished up quickly and be home already. Fighting feelings of disappointment, they headed out of the bustling little settlement and followed the beaten trail back toward their claims where they would settle themselves for another night alone in that immense new land.

# Chapter 6

## Homecoming

*Hello, Dear Emmaline,*
*It is starting to get dark, and*
*Papa has still not returned! I know*
*that Mama can't help but worry*

*although she tries not to let me see.
Here it is Thursday, and we are
getting ready to spend our fourth
night in our new home in this
territory. Today will make three long
days since the men all left to go
register in Guthrie. All the women,
just like Mama, are trying not to let
each other know that they are
wondering if something could have
gone wrong. We and our new
neighbors have kept busy. We are still
doing little things around our
campsites trying to be ready when
they get back to help get our homes
ready. We have continued to cut
blocks of sod and stack them on each
claim so they will be ready for the
men to build our shelters quickly
when they return. The children and I
take buckets of water around each
day and sprinkle them to keep them
from drying out.*

*Oh, Emmaline, where oh
where can they be? Mama and I have
prayed constantly for God to keep
them safe and bring them home soon.
But where are they? ...*

As the darkness deepened, Rebecca Jane
finished her note to Emmaline and replaced the
cover on her beautiful fountain pen. She could hear

faintly in the distance, the lonesome sound of the train whistle as the evening train from the north went chugging along the tracks. As she gazed up at the sky, Rebecca Jane couldn't resist the impulse to think, "If someone got off the train in town, it might take 30 minutes to get the horses and wagon from the livery, and another hour to drive here from there. She mentally calculated the time that a man might take to get home, just in case he had just come in on that train. She glanced at her mother and could tell that she was doing the same thing.

The two put on a cheerful front while watching the night sky and estimating the passing time. When it was undeniably obvious that Daniel had not been on that train, Rachel stretched and covered a yawn. "Well, I guess it is time we got to bed. There is still a lot of work we can do here tomorrow. It will be Friday; surely your father will get here then."

They unrolled their bedrolls in the wagon, put on their nightgowns, and crawled between the blankets. In spite of their worries, the fatigue from the fresh air and hard work soon overtook them and they drifted into a sound sleep.

Friday dawned clear and bright in the new settlers camp. Rachel and Rebecca Jane rose with the sun and looked around them. They were greeted by the now-familiar sight of tents and the white hooped covers on the wagons. While the two stood there breathing deeply of the sweet morning air, they watched the canvas covers waving gently in the morning breeze.

Rachel went to work stirring up the coals they had buried from last night's fire while Rebecca Jane filled the pot and put on the water for coffee. Rachel cut one of the precious oranges they had found in the Carpenters' store on their Wednesday trip into town. She and Rebecca each enjoyed half the orange while waiting for the oatmeal to cook. As they waited, the two discussed the tasks she had in mind for the day.

After they had eaten breakfast in the quiet of the morning, Rebecca began cleaning up the dishes, being very careful of their limited water. They had refilled their barrels from one of the two wells in Norman when they went in on Wednesday, but that was now running low.

"I sure wish we had a well with our own water right over there." Rebecca Jane pointed to a spot about twenty feet behind the wagon. "I will sure be glad when Papa and the other men get back and can take care of going to town to refill our water barrels. It is awfully hard to manage them by ourselves," Rebecca Jane commented. "You know another thing I will be glad to have built?" she continued as she looked questioningly at her mother.

"There are so many things we need to have done, it is hard to think of what we miss the most," replied Rachel. "I am sure the men all have ideas about which is the most important. We need a shelter. That shouldn't take long with the blocks we have already cut. It shouldn't take much more work to have a spot for a garden either. We can use the spot where we have been digging sod, and with just a little more plowing it will be ready for the garden. I am also looking forward to the time when we can have our own well. That may take hiring a crew to come out with more equipment than we have. "

"I think we could almost finish turning the garden over with a shovel and get that started right away," said Rebecca. "I want to plant some corn, and some peas, and some green beans."

"Not so fast," laughed her mother. "It's not even May yet. It's going to be hard enough growing anything this first year, but we sure don't want to plant too early and get everything frozen."

"But even more than any of those, I will be glad when Papa gets us an outhouse built. We're not supposed to talk about those things, but I am so tired of having to go off into the bushes! Especially when there aren't many bushes to be found!" Rebecca looked imploringly at her mother hoping for some sign that she agreed.

"You are so right!" said her mother emphatically. "You have no idea how important an outhouse is until you don't have one. If it is built right and taken care of correctly, it is so much more sanitary than going off into the bushes. And your Papa does know how to build it and take care of it!" Rachel looked around the campsite for a while as if considering, then continued, "Let's vote for the outhouse to be the first thing they build."

"I also hope that by next year, maybe some well-digging businesses will have come to town and maybe we will have enough money to have that done," added Rachel. "It would be wonderful to have our own well and not have to go to town to carry water back every few days?"

"Even just one here in the neighborhood to share would be so nice," said Rebecca thoughtfully

Passing the time with dreams of the home their family would make, the two had soon finished their work. With the campsite now neat and tidy, they walked across the fields of blowing grass to visit with their friends. Rebecca gathered up the children and took them to start a game of tag while their mothers visited and enjoyed another cup of coffee. Mary Annette Bridges was just learning to take her first few steps and tried valiantly to keep up with Brewster Groggins and the other children. They didn't understand the game, but were having fun, giggling when Rebecca let them catch her. Then they would turn around and run laughing, right into the arms of their pursuers!

After the women had shared the rest of the coffee from Jannetta Bridges' coffee-pot they poured cool drinks of water for the children when they ran up breathless and ready for a rest. The conversation ranged from when the men should be back, to how soon they should plant a garden, to what could be keeping the men, to how nice it would be to get an outhouse built, and again to what could possibly be keeping the men so long.

As the sun climbed up the curve of the bright blue bowl of the sky, the families parted to return to their own camps. There were beans to put on to cook, potatoes to peel, and a dozen other small chores necessary to prepare a meal on an open fire.

As the sun reached its peak and started down the other side of the sky, Rachel and Rebecca finished their meal and began to clean up for the second time that day.

"I think I will cover these things and keep them warm," said Rachel, "Surely your father will be here soon, and he is certain to be hungry."

"Yes, surely he will be," agreed Rebecca. "I hope he won't be gone for the whole weekend!"

Rebecca had gotten out her Emmaline journal and was so absorbed in reading through the thoughts she had recorded earlier that she was completely oblivious to anything around her. Suddenly, she heard her mother cry out while pointing off to the southwest. There, they could just see the outline of a wagon being pulled briskly along by a team of horses. The rising cloud of dust was making it very difficult to tell anything about it, but for some reason, all the women and their children were now running toward it. There seemed to be no doubt in any of their minds about who was in that wagon.

When the team was pulled to a halt, the five men jumped out to be greeted with much excitement. The air was filled with cries of, "Why did it take so long?" "I was just about ready to get worried," "You just can't imagine what it was like up in Guthrie," "Did you bring me anything, Papa?" "We've been digging sod bricks," and finally, "Got anything to eat, we're starved?"

The food was brought from all the campsites, reheated, and soon all were settled around eating and eagerly waiting to hear the stories to be told by the returning men.

Daniel stood up and looked around the group, "That was a mighty fine meal. But here it is barely past noon, and we have been sitting around for almost three days wishing we were back here so we could get busy on the work to be done. I think that talk about our adventures will have to wait until this evening."

"Can't waste this good daylight and the energy of five men who are just itching to get to work," put in Samuel.

The men seemed to have an agreement that Charles would be the first to have the five of them work on his claim. They mysteriously refused to tell the reason, just telling the women, "That's part of a long story. Time for stories will be later this evening!"

The women showed the men around the claims, proudly displaying the stacks of sod on each site. They told about working together to dig them and diligently sprinkling the piles with water each day so they wouldn't dry out before being used. The men were all properly impressed by what had been accomplished in their absence.

"My women are telling me that our most important need to be more civilized is a nice outhouse! I agree, so I vote we start with the outhouses first," said Daniel, looking around at his friends.

"Once we decide where to put them, some of us can start digging while the others drive back into town to get the materials. I am sure the water is running low and we will also need to fill the water barrels again. These pioneer women have saved us a lot of time on the shelters with these bricks already cut!" said young Harvey Miller clearly proud of Marian's part in the women's accomplishment.

"We won't need more than just a little while to build our shelters and a little more plowing will make a pretty good garden space for each of us," put in Samuel. "I sure am glad you ladies were all thinking ahead and gave us such a good start on our work!"

"We just wanted to do whatever we could to be sure we were ready for a day of rest on Sunday so we can all go into town for the hymn singing and prayer meeting," said Miranda Groggins, beaming happily at her husband.

Since the men all agreed that Charles, had the right to have his claim worked on first, they began to ask him where he would like to locate his privy.

Charles grinned in embarrassment as he said, "You fellows have all built these before and have a better idea than I do where it should go. Let's dig the others first. All of you have families here to consider, and there is just one of me. Maybe by the time we build the other four, I will know where mine should go."

The men agreed that they should start right then with the Bridges' claim which was close to the center of the five claims. They would dig the first outhouse there and then move on to the Simpsons, then the Groggins, the Millers, and finally, Charles Cunningham.

"Let's go get started," said Daniel. "After three days of doing nothing, I'm raring to go!"

After some conferencing, the men decided that Daniel, Harvey, and Charles, would stay there to decide on the locations and get started digging. Samuel and Robert would put the barrels in the wagons and make the trip into town for water and building supplies. Samuel, with his farming experience, had taken part in building many an outhouse during his growing-up years in Arkansas. He knew pretty much just what lumber and other equipment they would need.

Before Robert and Samuel went to gather the water-barrels and get the teams ready to go, the group toured the five claims and decided on good locations for each outhouse--keeping in mind the relation to where they planned to build the house and where the water well would be dug. With that decided, the three that were staying there grabbed picks, shovels, buckets, and other tools that might be useful. Those tools included a seven-foot ladder that Daniel had brought with him all the way from Missouri strapped firmly to the side of his wagon box. It would come in handy now! They headed for the Bridges' claim and the site for the first outhouse.

Robert and Samuel departed for town with one wagon loaded with the empty water barrels and another empty wagon to carry back the lumber and supplies they would buy.

The men first marked off a square about four and one-half feet on each side. From inside this square, they dug a layer of sod bricks and stacked them off to the side. then they marked off a square about three feet on each side in the center of the cleared area. Daniel and Harvey took their shovels and began digging inside the small square and placing the dirt into buckets. Charles took two buckets at a time to dump them on the garden site where the sod had been cut out earlier. The women agreed heartily with this as it gave them fresh dirt which would only need a quick plowing to make the garden ready to plant.

The digging went pretty quickly as the ground was still damp from the rain on Sunday. Soon the hole was too deep for two men to work there, and Daniel climbed out while Harvey continued digging. As the hole got deeper, a rope was tied to the bucket to haul it out of the pit.

Janetta soon came out with a pitcher of water and some glasses for the men. She poured for them all while they took a breather. She was so delighted with the progress, that she could no longer resist getting into the work.

After taking the pitcher back to her wagon, she returned to the digging site. "I think that if I could cut and carry sod bricks when we were here alone, I can surely carry a bucket of dirt. How about I carry the buckets and the other two of you can go on to start on the next one?"

All three of the men stopped and surveyed their work. Harvey was a pretty tall man, and the hole was now about up to his waist.

"We need to have it a little more than five feet," said Daniel as he straightened. "About your shoulder height, Harvey should be about right. It shouldn't take much longer on this one. How about you take a digging break, and I will take over here while Janetta carries the buckets? You and Charles can go mark off the next one and get the digging started."

By this time all the women and children were at the digging site. Everybody pitched in to carry as much as they were able. It was hard work for all, but the spirit of cooperation and fellowship was high. Laughter filled the air as the women worked and chatted while Rebecca took the children off to play a game. In a surprisingly short amount of time, when Daniel stood up and his head was just barely over the edge of the pit, he pronounced it deep enough. Rachel brought the ladder and Daniel climbed out. So, the work continued until the second pit was pronounced deep enough and the third was about two feet deep.

Just as they prepared to take a short rest, the wagons arrived back from town loaded with water, lumber, and other supplies.

They made quick work of unloading the lumber and supplies. The water barrels were delivered to all the campsites and, after long drinks of cool water, they were ready to get back to work on the outhouses. In the interest of having at least one privy complete and usable, they decided to build the houses for the two that were already dug first, before continuing with the digging.

Again, the spirit of teamwork was in the air, with the five men as well as the four wives all

working together. The men measured the wood and
prepared to cut the pieces to size. The women put on
gloves to protect their hands from the splinters and
soon were carrying boards to where they were
needed. They held boards in place, while the men
used the saw or hammered in nails. The afternoon
quickly slipped away, and as the sun began to slide
down the western sky, the women slipped away to
prepare food for the evening.

By the time twilight was beginning to cover
the territory, one of the outhouses was complete and
the second was well underway. Two more pits were
ready for their work to continue tomorrow.

"Looks like quitting time to me," said
Samuel. "I think we have made up for our three days
of doing nothing!"

Harvey surveyed the work they had
completed and nodded with satisfaction. "At the rate,
we are going, it looks like we will easily finish
tomorrow and have some time to start on the
shelters," he said.

As soon as the tired workers had consumed
the hearty meal that had been set out on planks
placed across some chairs, a large fire was built
where the friends could gather. The families made
themselves comfortable as they settled back for
conversation.

"It sure feels good to be home," said Harvey
stretching out while leaning on a pile of pillows with
his feet pointed toward the fire.

"And did anyone notice how easy it is to
already see this land as home?" mused Daniel as he

also stretched and leaned back.

"Come on, Papa," said Rebecca impatiently, as she snuggled in beside her parents, "You promised your story now. It's time!"

All the women and children raised their voices in agreement. "Come on now," Rebecca hit her father gently in the chest. "Don't stall, we are ready to hear your story." The men nodded their heads and looked to Daniel to begin. He began the account of all that had happened while a rapt audience of their families listened eagerly.

# Chapter 7

## The Long Days in Guthrie

*Hello, Dear Emmaline,*
*        After our long, long wait and*
*all our worries, it seems like since*
*Papa and the other men are back,*

77

*everything is all right again! It was*
*true that it was a long story, and we*
*all sat around the campfire late into*
*the night. The little children and the*
*babies fell asleep in their parents'*
*laps, but still, we all listened as they*
*told of their experiences in Guthrie.*
*They told us all about their long wait,*
*and how hard it had been waiting*
*there and knowing of all the work*
*they wanted to be doing here at home!*
*    As they told their story, we*
*understood that the days away had*
*been hard for them just as they had*
*been for us. I know that I shall not*
*forget it all the rest of my life! And,*
*Emmaline, I must tell it here as well*
*as I can remember...*

On Tuesday morning, April 23, Roger Harris
had pulled his wagon up in front of the depot while
his five friends climbed down. They had arrived
early that morning at his temporary livery stable to
have their team and wagon cared for while they were
away. After thanking Roger profusely for bringing
them back to the depot, they joined the crowd
already waiting and looking eagerly to the south. The
whistle could be heard faintly in the distance and the
waiting passengers began to line up to board the train
as soon as it would arrive.

In a few more minutes the engine came
roaring in pulling several passenger cars. They had

boarded the train and looked around for five seats together. It appeared that many others had the same idea, that riding the train would help to get their registration done faster and get them back to their land and their families. The men searched from car to car and finally found two wide seats where the five of them could sit across from each other and share a little conversation as the train labored along taking them up the tracks to Guthrie.

Robert Bridges gazed out the window, watching the scene move by outside. "It may not be awfully fast, but it sure beats trying to get up there in a wagon!"

"Well, so far since I left Arkansas City, I rode the train from Kansas, I walked right up to the river heading into the territory, and I would have walked all the rest of the way if you hadn't come along!" the youngest of the group, Charles, spoke with a grin. "I can tell you the train sure beats walking!" He looked around the little group and his expression gave evidence of his thanks that he had happened onto such a fine group of friends.

The train got underway and as they moved along, they could see tents, wagons, and freshly built sod houses clustered along the edges of the tracks with some that were more scattered farther off in the distance. Children ran and played through the prairie grass. Here and there a dog ran excitedly with them as the children threw sticks to be fetched. This land, which had been empty of activity just yesterday, now was a bustling settlement full of resolute pioneers.

The train moved along slowly, causing some

comments from the riders. "I'm not sure but what we might have made just as good time in a wagon," said Harvey.

"Well," put in Daniel, "I guess if I were driving this train with all those animals and people so close to the tracks, I might go a little slow, too."

They all watched for a while, in wonder at the lack of fear shown by the people and animals along the tracks. Finally, they settled back into their seats just as the train slowed even more. The wheels began to squeal and scream along the tracks as the train slowed gradually to a stop. The conductor came through the car calling out "Verbeck Station."

As the train slowly ground to a halt, those on board remained firmly in their places. The doors were opened and more people, mainly roughly clad men and a few women, crowded quickly into the already packed cars.

"Did he say 'Verbeck'?" Charles Cunningham asked, looking questioningly to his friends.

"Sure sounded like it," they all agreed.

"I ran into a fellow while I was waiting in Kansas. He was waiting until time to come into the territory just like I was. Anyway, he said he was from Verbeck, Kansas," said Charles, frowning hard to remember. "He said he had an uncle that came to the territory a couple of years ago to work at a station for the railroad and he started calling the place Verbeck after his hometown in Kansas. I remembered the uncle's name because it was Charles, like mine------only it was Charles

Chamberlain," he nodded, pleased with himself for remembering, then finished triumphantly, "Guess this might be that place."

Harvey Miller was peering out the dirty window for a better view of the small water stop. "Look over there," he said pointing. "That boxcar has a sign on it. Looks like M...O...O...R...E. You think, maybe they're going to call this place Moore?"

"Nah!" a man spoke up from the seat behind them. "That's just another employee of the railroad. His name's Al Moore. He's been living there a couple or so years. He just put his name out there to be sure he got his mail delivered to him. Worked for the railroad for a while myself, then quit that job so I could get in the run and get myself some land. That's how I happen to know about him. Who would ever call a town Moore, anyway?"

Someone nearby said, just loud enough to be heard over the rattling of the car, "Now Verbeck, there's a name you can remember!"

Samuel Groggins shook his head and said quietly to his friends, "Don't know about that. I guess everybody hears differently."

His friends chuckled quietly as Robert Bridges finished his thought for him, "Somehow it doesn't seem to me that Verbeck has much of a ring to it."

By now the car was vastly overfilled. Men were standing in the aisles and hanging onto the backs of the seats nearest to them. It was obvious from their comments that all shared a common goal of getting to Guthrie as soon as they could.

There was another stop at Oklahoma Station, where only a few of the waiting, would-be passengers were able to squeeze aboard. From the open window, those on the train overheard the loud protests as the conductor called out to those still waiting, "No more room. There'll be another train along soon." The train crept on. It moved slowly through a station called Edmond, and finally, the conductor came through calling, "Guthrie next stop. Fifteen minutes."

The only thing the men had brought with them was a basket with a few sandwiches, so they grabbed it and quickly looked around them, preparing to leave. All were now gazing out the windows with new interest, hoping for the first sight of the Guthrie station. The sun was high in the sky as the train screeched and rattled, slowing down until it finally came to a shuddering stop. In the sudden quiet the men stood, ready to make their way out of the railway car. After the time spent on the train, they found themselves speaking in unnaturally loud voices. "Guess we need to go find where the registration office is," shouted Daniel.

The conductor laughed as he spoke to them, "It's not far from here. They could probably hear you from here just now! It's just a little way over there," he said pointing off to the east of the tracks. "You can't miss it. That's where everybody's going."

Harvey, Robert, Daniel, Charles, and Samuel climbed down from the train, took a quick look around, and headed east following the crowd who were all going in the same direction. A short distance from the depot, they passed a lot filled with 40 to 50 small tents. A man in denim jeans, a shiny vest, and a string tie was busily writing on a pad of paper the names of those who stopped at his lot. After collecting some coins or bills from them, he would point them to one of the tents. There was a crude sign fastened to a tent pole announcing, "Santa Fe House." The man was loudly proclaiming to those on their way to the registration office, about the comforts of staying in his establishment while waiting to register their claims.

The men shook their heads in amazement at this reckless squandering of money as they continued making their way to a small unpainted building with a tall, bare false-front. It seemed that every square inch of the field in front of the building was filled with people milling about. On closer examination, they could see a pattern to the way the people were standing. The long line wound back and forth around the open area in front of the door, taking advantage of the shade of the few little trees while still filling the field to capacity.

The five men walked along searching for the end of the line. They soon observed that in preparing Guthrie to be one of the two registration offices for the new territory, little provision had been made to provide necessities for the thousands of people who were now there. The story going through the crowd was that they were barely able to finish a structure for the land office before they needed to open the doors. The bare front might have been intended to hold a sign designating it as "land office," but that hardly seemed necessary since one would have to look a long way to find another building of any kind. Those who had thought of preparations had seen it only in a commercial sense and were there with their wares shouting out to offer them for sale at outrageous prices.

They joined the line which was slowly inching back and forth across the field, while constantly adding more eager people to the line behind them. They stood there looking around in despair.

"Might as well make yourselves comfortable," said a man nearby who was leaning back against a small twisted oak tree. "I've been here since yesterday afternoon, and I still have a ways to go. I thought surely since I got here so quick, I would get right on through."

"It's hard for me to see how anyone could stake a claim and get here by the time the door opened at noon yesterday. But some were here!" put in another man. "I suspect some of them didn't get here that fast by doing it all legally."

"It's pretty sure that not everybody waited until noon to start their run yesterday," observed an old gentleman with a long bushy gray beard.

Here and there groups were lounging on the ground playing cards while holding their places in the line. A few were reading newspapers or dime novels. Since not everybody had thought to bring something to amuse themselves, a brisk trade soon developed for exchanging books, newspapers, or decks of cards. Those who had brought books or something to pass the time, were trading among themselves or gladly taking a nickel or dime from those around them to pass on their materials when they were finished with them.

One group farther up in the line were all involved in either playing or watching a game of mumblety-peg. Good-natured cheers and jeers were heard as a group of men, standing around a circle drawn on the ground, waited to take their turns to compete in a variety of trick tosses of their pocket knives to land within the circle. After some time, the man with the fewest good tosses got down on his knees with loud protests and, after rooting around in the dirt inside the circle, came up with a small wooden peg between his teeth and dirt on his nose and chin. During this time, the line had moved a short distance, so the group moved along and redrew their circle. Different men claimed places around the circle while others returned to watching the game while still keeping their places in line.

Under a tree nearby, two men sat with low tables over their laps. A sign fastened to the tree above them read, "FILL OUT YOUR PAPERS, $5.00." They were doing a brisk business and had more customers waiting in line for their services.

As the group of friends reluctantly settled down on the ground to wait, Daniel looked around them at the many people gathered there and commented, "I sure wish we had known about this so that our families wouldn't be worrying when it takes us so long to get back."

Robert nodded his head in agreement, "Janetta is just a natural worrier, and she will be sure the worst has happened."

A man sitting nearby in the shade of a tree turned to them with a grin and said, "I think you all just discovered what the rest of us have already found out. Nobody's going to get here, file, and get back home in one day. We've already been here since yesterday afternoon. My son is up there in line holding our spot. We're trading off sitting over here in the shade for a while. I'll go in a little bit and stand while he comes over here to rest. Looks like he's getting pretty close now; we might even get finished before they close tonight."

"Well," said Robert, looking around at his friends, "It looks like we are here for a long stay."

The men shared among themselves the sandwiches they had brought and they drank thirstily from their canteens. "I guess we better conserve our water," observed Charles, "I haven't seen any sign of any more around to replace it."

"I am afraid we may get pretty hungry and cold, too, before the night is over," said Harvey with a shake of his head.

Daniel looked at the people in line around them. "Would you folks see it as cheating if some of us left long enough to go see if we can rustle up some blankets and some supper for our group tonight? Would we lose our places in line?"

People around them smiled and shook their heads. One answered, "I reckon sooner or later, we're all going to have to leave our places for a while, whether it's nature, or food, or water that's calling us."

Another added, "Looks like we're all going to be neighbors here in this territory; might as well start out by acting neighborly."

Robert looked back toward the train tracks and offered, "I'll be glad to go scout around to see what we can find if you want me to."

"I'll go too," put in Harvey.

The others nodded their heads and reached into their pockets to give Robert some of their remaining cash to get whatever he might find to keep them warm and fed through the cool spring night.

As their friends walked away, Daniel, Samuel, and Charles prepared to wait. They seated themselves on the ground at their place in line and tried to get comfortable.

Samuel took off his jacket and rolled it up. He lay down on the ground, with the jacket under his head and his hat over his face. "Well, it was an early morning, especially after Brewster was awake most of the night. I could sleep on a bed of rocks," he said as he closed his eyes. "Wake me when we move up in line."

The others settled down to while away the afternoon. Charles picked up a branch that had fallen off a nearby tree. He began to whittle away with his pocket knife and, before long, he had produced a small whistle. It made a high shrill sound when he blew into it. He then found a larger branch and repeated the process. He continued to work on that one, making several small holes along the length of it. Soon when he put it to his mouth, he was able to play a series of musical notes. After a bit of experimentation and practice, he was able to produce a barely recognizable version of *"Yankee Doodle"* and many voices joined in to sing along with gusto. After a bit more practice, the tune of *"Dixie"* was greeted enthusiastically and the same settlers joined in the singing.

Before long, Robert and Harvey returned with arms loaded. They put the load on the ground and began to show their treasures. There were five warm blankets, a large jug of water, a round chunk of cheese, some bread, and a large bag of peanuts.

"Looks like just what we are going to need," said Daniel, "We shouldn't freeze or starve."

The afternoon passed slowly, with every minute seeming to stretch on and on. As the huge glowing ball of the sun was approaching the horizon, a man stepped out of the door of the office, and called out, "That's all for today. Open again early tomorrow morning." The announcement was greeted by a chorus of groans, and people began to seat themselves and roll up in their coats or blankets.

Slowly the twilight fell, and overhead, the breathtaking light show of millions of stars began to twinkle through the darkness. Those waiting out there on the prairie were in awe of the beauty.

"Wow! I never saw a sky look like this back in Missouri," said Daniel quietly.

Harvey Miller, sighed with his eyes fixed on the sky, "This is the first time Marian and I have

been separated since we were married! I wonder if
the sky looks this beautiful back there at Norman. I
bet she is looking at that big, fat lopsided moon and
thinking of me just the same as I am here thinking of
her!"

Quiet gradually descended upon the hundreds
of people waiting there. In the peaceful evening,
crickets chirped rhythmically, and birds could be
heard calling softly. Here and there could be heard
the rustling and shuffling of a huge crowd settling
down. Soon, the only sounds disturbing the quiet
were snores rising into the cool night air. The hardy
pioneers had settled in to await the dawn of a new
day which would bring them that much closer to
making a reality of their dreams for new lives here in
this huge unsettled territory.

\*\*\*\*

Wednesday morning, April 24, had dawned
in Guthrie with a beautiful clear sky arched
overhead. The hundreds of settlers woke to find
themselves covered with dampness from a light dew
that had fallen. No one seemed to care, however, as
they stood, stretched, and looked around getting their
bearings and remembering why they were there.

Robert and Daniel were the first to wake in
their little circle of five and with the sounds of
movement around them, the others soon began to
rouse themselves.

"Well, good to see you this beautiful
morning," said Daniel laughing as young Charles

rubbed his eyes and yawned widely. Charles' brown hair was standing out at all angles giving him a wild appearance.

"What's so funny?" asked Charles as he ran his fingers through his wild hair making it even wilder.

They stood and shook out their blankets and coats. The coats felt good against the spring morning chill. They folded and stacked the blankets near their place in the long line.

Charles looked off across the hundreds of people looking like ants in an anthill as they woke and began to move around. "Looks like it may take a pretty long walk to find a bush to give a little privacy to answer nature's call," he observed. "I think I may go off that way," he said pointing.

"Guess I'll go that way too," said Harvey, "We can take turns holding the places in line. Be back soon."

As they left, the others gazed around. "Wonder if there's anyone around this morning selling eats," said Samuel, "I could sure use something."

Robert shaded his eyes and pointed, "That man over there has a big basket on his arm. That might be what he is doing."

Daniel turned to look the same direction, "I think you just might be right," he said, "We'll have to check on him."

By the time all the men had returned from their morning walks, there were several people walking around the grounds carrying large baskets.

Harvey caught the attention of one of them and waved him over. He opened his basket to reveal inside, a smaller basket full of hard-boiled eggs; there was also bread, cheese, and a bag of small red apples.

"You can make a fine breakfast from these," he told them, "and these apples! They may not look so good, but they are from my last year's crop over in Arkansas. I kept them stored in a nice cool cellar all winter. They have a mighty sweet flavor!"

The men all chose their breakfasts from his wares, paid him with a few of their remaining coins, and settled down in line to enjoy their food.

"Um-umm, he was right! Those apples do taste mighty good!" said Daniel as he bit into his apple.

"I sure hope we don't have to stay too much longer, or my money might run out!" said Charles jingling a handful of coins before putting them back in his pocket.

"I think that is true for everybody," put in Robert, "None of us expected to have to stay this long."

At about that time the door to the registration office was opened from the inside and two men stepped out.

One of them shouted for attention trying to make himself heard above the noise of the crowd. As people began to notice him, the noise gradually subsided until the man was finally able to be heard.

"Starting now," he said, "We are going to give each of you a number to show your place in line. We will call numbers as we are ready for you. We regret that you are having to wait so long, but with this method, you can at least walk around without losing your place."

With that, the other man began moving down the line giving each person a slip of paper. The five friends were far away from the door, and it took quite a while to get to them.

"Look how high this number is!" said Harvey, "We may be here all week!"

"Wow! I sure wish we had some way to let our families know what's going on," said Samuel shaking his head.

"I'm sure they will have a pretty good idea," said Daniel. "They know there were a lot of people that came in on Monday, so they know that there will be a lot up here trying to register."

"Maybe we can find a little more comfortable spot, now anyway," said Robert as they began to walk away. They moved over to a spot shaded slightly by one of the stunted little trees. They all sat down and made themselves as comfortable as possible while preparing for another day's long wait.

During the endless morning, the sun climbed slowly up in the sky. For something to do, they walked around the grounds visiting with others and sharing stories of why they had come to the Territory.

The day dragged slowly on. The men began to amuse themselves by counting how many minutes passed between called numbers. Sometimes it would be five minutes, sometimes fifteen, and sometimes thirty. With some mental arithmetic, they would guess how long before they were called. Their estimates did not show much promise of accuracy since the length of time between calls varied widely. Some of the guesses varied from Thursday morning to Friday or even later.

"I guess the paperwork on some of the claims is more complicated than others," said Daniel shaking his head.

The men were all accustomed to constant hard work and spending hours at a time pacing around was not their choice of how to spend the day. They began to take longer walks without fear that the process might suddenly speed up and catch them unaware. They put all five of their numbers in an envelope together and one of them agreed to stay near the registration office while the others ventured out, exploring farther away to escape the unavoidable inactivity.

"Never thought I would see the time when I would wish I could go out and do a good long day's work," commented Robert as he arrived back from his exploring.

"Maybe we can remember this in July and August when we are out working in the field," said Daniel as he handed over the envelope and prepared to leave for his exercise.

"Four hundred, ninety-five," called the agent from the door.

Robert couldn't help checking inside the envelope although he knew perfectly well what numbers were in there, and that nothing would have changed. "Enjoy your walk," he said, then with a grin, he added, "You might want to check on Charles while you are out. I guess he looks like the handsome, eligible young bachelor he is, and a group of single women had him cornered over there. He may need rescuing!"

Daniel laughed heartily and waved as he started off for his turn of exploring.

So, in this way, the long afternoon and evening dragged on. As it got a little later, the men all thought that the time between calls seemed shorter.

"They might have gotten another helper in there," speculated Harvey.

"Or maybe, after a little practice, they are getting better at what they are doing," put in Charles who had indeed managed to politely escape from his group of admirers with his good manners intact!

As darkness descended, the agents came out on the steps and called out, "That is all for today. Keep your numbers and we will start tomorrow morning where we left off."

"About 200 more numbers before they get to ours," moaned Samuel looking at the paper he was holding.

"Do you think they'll even get to us tomorrow?" Charles asked the others.

"Well, it seems to me that they went through more than 200 today," said Daniel scratching his head.

"Hey, I have an idea," said Harvey with a smile. "We have all agreed that we will work together to get the big jobs done on our claims, right?" The others all nodded in agreement as they listened.

"So, we will each make our best guess as to when we will all be registered and ready to leave. We write them all down and put them in another envelope. Then when we head for the train, we take them out and whoever guessed the closest to the time will be the first to get his place worked on, next closest will be next and so on. That will add a little interest to our wait," said Harvey with a grin.

The others laughed about the idea, but all took out pencils and paper to start figuring what their guess would be. By the time the guesses were all in the envelope, it was fully dark except for the moon and stars overhead. As they had the night before, they all rolled up in their rented blankets and tried to make themselves as comfortable as possible for Wednesday night, their third night in the Unassigned Lands and their second in Guthrie.

The men had whiled away another long, boring day on Thursday, and the office doors were closed after numbers were called up to about ten before those held by the men. Feeling a little more optimistic, they had all settled in for one more night rolled up on the ground in their rented blankets. Sure enough, on Friday morning, their numbers were called within the first hour after the office opened. All had their information well in order and had quickly filled out their papers to get their claims registered. The agents didn't seem at all bothered by Charles filing as the head of household for his sick mother and his two sisters since he had the papers verifying that status.

In a very short time, they found themselves back on the train, heading south. The tracks seemed to stretch on endlessly as they were all eager to be back with their families. As soon as they were on the train, they had checked the envelope to see who had guessed the closest. Charles had predicted that they would all be ready to leave by 5:00 p.m. on Thursday while the others had all guessed earlier times, so he had won the right to have the group work on his place first.

****

With the mystery solved about what had happened in those three days in Guthrie and why they were all insisting that Charles was entitled to have the first work done on his farm, the friends picked up their sleeping children and moved away toward their own claims. They were eagerly looking forward to a rewarding day of work on the coming Saturday.

# Chapter 8

## Praising God in a New Land

*Hello, Dear Emmaline,*
*It is now Sunday afternoon,*
*and what a wonderful day it has*
*been! We all got up, had breakfast*

*and dressed in our best clothes to go
into Norman for church! All of our
neighbors came along since they
didn't know of anyone from any of
their churches who were meeting yet.
It was so beautiful! We all met on Mr.
Streeter's lot close to the area they
are calling downtown. The singing
was beautiful, and the scripture
reading and discussion of the
scripture were so inspiring. I think
everyone felt grateful to God for
leading us here. There are such
exciting things going on as we get
settled into this town and our church.
I think this is going to be a very good
place to live...*

The Simpson family had invited Charles to
accompany them to Norman that Sunday morning to
the meeting being held by members of the Methodist
Episcopal Church, South. Daniel had removed the
cover from the wagon since they had now put up a
tent and did not need to sleep in the wagon anymore.
Some of the crates were placed in the wagon to sit
on, and the hoops had also now been taken off. They
looked forward to enjoying the delightfully fresh
spring air on their pleasant ride to town.

Rachel and Rebecca came from the house
dressed in their best Sunday dresses anticipating the
worship they would share, and the friends they
would see. While Daniel helped Rachel to get into

the wagon, Charles turned to Rebecca with an exaggerated bow, held out his hand and said, "Your carriage awaits, my lady."

Rebecca was startled since she usually just climbed up the wheel and got herself in any way she could. Somehow now, with her best Sunday dress on, and a gracious young gentleman there offering his hand, climbing up the wheel just didn't seem right. She returned his bow with a curtsy of her own and with his help, climbed primly into the wagon and took her seat on one of the boxes. Charles promptly climbed in and sat on the box beside her.

When they arrived at the lot where the singing would be held, they found many of the friends who had shared with them the drive up to Downing's Crossing. They also saw many new friends that they had met since then. The gathering was an inspiring time of hymn singing, praying and Bible reading. Charlotte Carpenter again took the lead in the music, her clear soprano voice ringing out in the brisk early morning air. As she started hymn after hymn, the group would enthusiastically join in. The minister who had been sent to the territory to claim the church site was there. He did not preach or lead the service, but he did tell them that they would be visited soon by officials of the Methodist Episcopal Church, South who would assist in organizing a real congregation of those who wanted to be a part of it.

The railroad stop of Norman Station was quickly becoming just Norman, the town, and it looked like everyone in that new town who felt like offering a little thanks and praise had come to the hymn singing. Although people came from many denominations, they made a congenial group as they gathered. Their friends from Downing's Crossing were all there, and they were able to spend some time catching up on the happenings in their lives. All too soon, the service was finished and it was time to head back to their new homes. Rachel invited Charles to join their family for Sunday lunch, and he accepted with pleasure.

Again, the ladies were helped into the wagon and soon they were on the way home still enjoying a feeling of joy from the service. As they rode along, Rebecca sat puzzling over some things she had noticed during the morning. Finally, she said, "I don't understand, Papa. Why are there two kinds of Methodist Episcopal Church? Why is the church of the Millers different than ours?"

Daniel pondered the question for a while and began, "Well Rebecca, that goes back quite a while." He frowned in thought as he worked at remembering. "You've heard Pastor Williams back in Missouri talk about how John Wesley didn't really intend to start a new church when he was in England, and he began to meet with a group of young men, students who wanted to study the Bible together. Well, since they had their own methodical style of Bible study, they were soon being called Methodists. When America was being settled, naturally the people wanted churches, and the new Methodists were one of the churches that came. After American Methodists separated from the Church of England, they came to be called the Methodist Episcopal Church."

Rachel took up the story, "The church had pretty well spread throughout the states by the time the Revolutionary War was over. Then, along in the early 1800s about 1828 or so, questions about slavery started coming up every four years at their general conferences," Rachel paused and looked back at Rebecca. "It seems that one of their leaders, a bishop I think, had come to own some slaves when he married a woman who owned them."

"Some of the churches didn't allow their ministers to be slave owners." continued Daniel. "So, he had a problem! Where he lived, it was illegal to buy or sell slaves. He couldn't legally sell them, but the church didn't want him to own them either! Well, the question kept coming back up through a good many years. Finally, in 1844, the Methodist Episcopal Church in the southern states left the main body and became the Methodist Episcopal Church, South. The discipline and rules of the south church were very similar to those of their old church except, you can be sure, they included some kind of solution for what to do about slave ownership."

Rebecca looked even more puzzled, "But that was years and years ago! The north and south fought a war about it! It has been settled now and no one can own or buy or sell slaves! Why are there still two different Methodist churches?"

"Well," continued Daniel slowly and thoughtfully, "When two churches have been separated for a while, they come to be a little different. Their beliefs about God and the Christian life may be pretty much alike, but little differences about how to interpret and live that life will have crept into their rules and discipline. Certain people have made attempts to get some talks started between the two churches. Representatives from the north conference have gone to visit the south conference and the south has visited the north but, so far, nothing has happened!"

"It will though," said Rachel, "But for right now, there will be two Methodist Churches in Norman. From the lot that our church has claimed, the corner just south and east  through the block has been claimed by the North Methodists."

"I think they have someone coming to do the organizing for the north church just like we do for ours. We are already planning for a building. You noticed the little building on the lot, I'm sure. They figure maybe it was used by the railroad crew for some of their workers. I talked to the minister this morning, and there are plans to use it and add on to it. We will have a place to meet in no time." said Daniel. "By cleaning it up good and adding on to it, we can have an adequate place for our congregation to meet right away. Some of us are meeting next Saturday to look it over and sketch up some plans. If the work on our claim comes along well enough, I will plan to work with them as many Saturdays as I can."

All the way back to the claim, Rebecca sat primly in her seat feeling very adult as the four of them discussed plans for their new church in this town that was now their new home. When they arrived at their claims, Charles again, with exaggerated politeness, bowed as he assisted her from the wagon "May I take your hand, my Lady?"

Going along with his joke, she made her own deep curtsy and said, "Thank you, Sir Charles!"

Daniel and Charles went to take care of the horses, leaving Rebecca and Rachel in privacy to change from their Sunday best into their everyday clothes. They quickly finished preparing the meal that had been left cooking in the coals from their fire, and soon the family, along with Charles, sat down to enjoy a leisurely meal together.

# Chapter 9

## Home Is Where You Make It

In the weeks that followed, the five families of neighbors and friends continued to work together from daylight to dark going from claim to claim finishing those necessary jobs to make these new claims into farms. Before long an outhouse was finished for each claim. The stacks of sod bricks had grown as the sod dug from the outhouse sites was cut up and added. The women and children sprinkled them with water daily to keep them from drying out before the men were ready to turn them into small sod houses.

Daniel brought out the small plow that he had kept tucked away in the wagon all the way from Missouri. With one of the horses hitched to it, in just a half-day's work he was able to turn a small garden plot where the bricks had been dug on each claim. The women and children worked on those spaces to prepare for their gardens. They had a good time visiting and planning together to have different vegetables in their gardens to be able to share so everyone could have some variety. They watered their plantings sparingly with some of the precious water brought from town in the water barrels. They all had rain-barrels sitting on their sites, but not a drop had come to fill them.

Little by little the men had managed to clear a small field for each of the five claims. They would continue taking a few morning hours out of each day to get a little planting done before starting the other major jobs they planned for the day.

That next job, very eagerly anticipated by the women, was the building of the sod houses to shelter the families. This job, however, had to be combined with all the other small jobs required to establish a new farm. They seldom had a complete day at a time to spend building. Still, they continued to make progress, even at this slower pace.

Knowing that they must be able to take advantage of even the short times available to work each day, enough materials had been purchased to start framing doors and windows for each of the houses. The question of panes to go in those window frames was something for which each family made their own plans. Two families believed glass windows were important enough to allocate money from their dwindling funds. The sheets of glass had been padded and packed carefully before transporting out to their farms and then they carefully stored them, waiting until their homes' walls were up. They planned to use them in their sod houses and then move them when they built their permanent homes. The other families would cover their windows with sheets of heavy paper which were coated with oil in order to let in more light and yet stand up to the rains that the farm families were expecting. They felt like they could wait until time for their permanent homes, before purchasing the glass panes.

To build each house, they had found a level spot and marked out a rectangle for the small house. This was where the walls would be. The crew then made quick work of removing a layer of sod from inside the marked walls and stacked the sod bricks with the others they had made earlier. Everyone was then called in to help in smoothing and packing down the area for the floor. Some used their heavy boots, and some used a flat board to smooth with. Even the children came to help, stomping the loose dirt and running around chasing each other! When the floor was pronounced firm and smooth enough, the children were free to go somewhere to play until their help was needed on the next floor.

After the floor was done, the walls were finished quickly. They stacked the sod, brick style, in straight rows along their markings. It wasn't long before they had the windows and doors framed with the lumber they had purchased in town. As they neared the required height for the walls, ladders were needed to continue laying the sod bricks; when buying supplies, they had known they would be needing more than one ladder, and they had bought extra lumber to build another one.

The roof was definitely the hardest part of the soddie. Supporting it presented a problem. None of them had felt like they would have to buy lumber to build the framework for the roof. A trip to the cross-timbers area resulted in a supply of slender tree trunks that could be used to build a latticework that would hold up a layer of sod. Some of them decided they no longer needed the canvas covers on their wagons, and they placed those over the latticework before covering it with sod. This provided a firm, nearly rainproof roof.

By the time the first house had reached this point, time was slipping away, and the men decided they should move on to the next house, turning the first one over to the women for the inside work.

Although none of the neighbors planned to be in the little houses very long, they also understood that there were many things that might happen to

delay the building of a permanent home. So, the
women worked hard on the inside of their temporary
homes to make them as comfortable as possible.
Even with the canvas covers from their wagons
underneath the sod of the roof, they could not help
being nervous about the possibility of insects or
worms coming from the sod ceiling or walls onto
their beds or kitchen tables. Looking for solutions,
they bought cheesecloth and plaster from the
Carpenters' store in town. They covered their
ceilings with a thin coat of plaster and then fastened
the cheesecloth tightly over that. This had an added
benefit of providing a nice light-colored ceiling that
made the inside look much brighter than it had. A
thin paste of plaster was also brushed on the walls
and any other bare sod spaces.

Rachel had brought along her treasured
sewing machine, and soon she was helping all her
neighbors to find usable materials to turn into
curtains for their windows, and rag rugs for the
floors. The small living spaces were becoming very
comfortable and pleasant looking.

By the time all were completed, it was well
into the hot days of the summer, and the crops on the
small lots planted at each farm were getting tall in
the fields. With all the shells of the houses up, the
women hurried to complete their finish work inside.

July was slipping away by the time all were
finished. The families viewed all the new homes
with satisfaction and celebrated by sharing an
outdoor pot-luck lunch together. Rachel looked with
satisfaction around the sod cabins and observed,

"Well, they all look good, but I don't want to get too comfortable and forget about getting a real house built." All the other women agreed that this was only a temporary solution.

Charles was pleased that they had included his home in their finishing and decorating. "This is just wonderful," he said. "I can't believe what you ladies can do with so little! I wonder if it might be time to go on up to Kansas and get my mom and sisters. I am really anxious to get them back here with me."

He looked around the circle of friends who had become so much like family to him, "With Mom so sick, I kind of begrudge any time we have to be apart. Do you suppose that it would be bad for her health to live here in the soddie?"

"Well, I'm no doctor, and I don't really know just how ill your mother is, but I have heard that often this kind of active life in the fresh air can turn out to be especially beneficial to one's health," said Rachel thoughtfully. "It seems to me that just the happiness and peace of mind of being here with all her family would make her feel better.

"Charlotte Carpenter told me that the word in town is that there will be a doctor here in town soon. She said there is an office already being prepared for him, so your mother would have access to medical care," contributed Janetta.

"Your two sisters will certainly be a big help taking care of your mom. I can help too, since we don't have any children yet," offered Marian Miller shyly.

"I am sure that if I were your mom, I would be so glad to get my family back together that I would be willing to put up with a lot of hardships," added Janetta Bridges.

The women were supportive of the idea to bring Mrs. Cunningham there as soon as possible and agreed to help Charles as much as they could with her care and making the home comfortable for her. With that, Charles' mind was made up and he began to make plans to go to Arkansas City as soon as possible.

# Chapter 10

## New Neighbors

*Hello, Dear Emmaline,*
*        It has been such a long week!*
*Mama, Papa and I took Charles to the*
*depot on Monday and Papa promised*

*that we would come back on Friday to
meet them when they return. Charles
has become so much like part of our
family that I get up in the mornings
and it just seems natural that I find
myself looking over to his house
hoping to see him there. Mama and I
stay so busy here. I would not have
imagined there could be so much to do
getting a new home and farm started!
Yesterday, we finished moving into our
house. I would never have believed
that a house built from chunks of sod
could look this nice! Yesterday I found
my doll, Sally, down behind a box I
was unpacking. She was still wearing
the clothes that I had put on her the
day of the run! I have kept so busy
with all the work, helping our
neighbors, and helping to care for
their children that I have not even
thought about dressing poor Sally for
life in the Unassigned Lands. I found
her box of clothes, put a more frontier
style dress on her and settled her
against a pillow on my bed. Now she
can observe my comings and goings
and all the work we are doing.
Emmaline, sometimes it seems
almost like I am a different girl than
the one that came here in that wagon
such a short time ago! I wonder, is this*

*what growing up means…*

On the Friday morning after Charles left to get his mother and sisters, Daniel hitched up the wagon while Rachel and Rebecca finished preparations for a trip into town. "Town" now included many rough wooden buildings and still some tents. Two hotels had now been built. The Planters hotel had been the first to be finished with the St. James hotel the next. Both included several rooms plus dining and cooking facilities.

There was such a wide variety of goods available by now that, if one had a little cash, most anything they needed could be found. Rachel and Rebecca found it exciting to wander from shop to shop replenishing a few of their staple supplies while being tempted by luxuries that they knew they could not afford yet. They promised themselves, though, *In a few years, when the crops start to come in!*

Daniel checked the train schedule to see when they might expect Charles. There were several trains scheduled for that day, so he planned that they would shop at the Carpenters' store, visit with their friends the Harrises at their new livery, and meet each arriving train. While Rachel and Rebecca were enjoying their shopping, Daniel explored the arrangements that had been made for mail delivery. In the middle of the floor in the depot waiting room, they had placed a large box, and in it were all the letters that had been delivered so far to the Norman area. Daniel looked through it, although he didn't think he was expecting anything for himself or his family. During his search, he found one for Mr. Charles Cunningham and made a mental note to be sure to tell Charles to pick it up when he arrived.

The day passed pleasantly as the family visited with their different friends, always arranging to be at the depot when a southbound train arrived. They were disappointed each time, and began to wonder if perhaps Charles and his family were not able to be ready to come today.

As evening approached, another train arrived from the north, and after much wheezing and screeching, finally came to a halt with a last big puff of steam. The Simpsons were all there watching as passengers began to unload from the cars.

While Rebecca Jane watched the people descending the steps, she played a game in her mind imagining what each person was here for. One man carrying a bag with tools sticking out of the top must have been looking for a place to settle. "*I wonder why he didn't get here for the run. I hope he is not too late to find a good place,*" she mused.

A well-dressed man came down the steps with a woman who was wearing a stylish dress and hat. The woman held the hand of a young boy about five or six years old. The man was probably a banker coming to set up a bank here in this new town. They would be building a fine house before long. A woman descended the stairs carrying a baby, and she was followed by two more children clinging to her skirts and peeking around her. Rebecca looked over the crowd and saw a man looking anxiously around.

He seemed to relax when he saw the woman with the children, and hurried up to them. Thus it went until it seemed everyone must be off the train.

Just then, two young girls came down the steps looking around uncertainly. One was several inches shorter than the other and had long blond hair while the taller one had short dark hair. Rebecca noted them briefly, thinking, *Charles said his sisters were twins. They must not have made this train.* She continued watching those descending the steps, but just as she was about to turn away, Charles appeared on the steps and turned to help bring a wheeled chair carefully down. After the chair was on the ground, he went back up the steps and carefully brought down a frail-looking woman whom he settled carefully into the chair. As the two girls she had seen earlier joined Charles, the Simpsons hurried over eagerly to welcome them.

Charles greeted them warmly and said, "It's so good of you to come to meet us. Don't know how we would have gotten home without you!"

The frail woman smiled at them and said, "I wish I could get up and greet you better. I am so thankful for how kind you have been to Charles."

Rebecca had been staring at the two girls with surprise and with a puzzled look at Charles, she blurted out, "But you said your sisters were twins!"

Charles laughed and looked to the girls who were giggling together.

"We are," said the blond girl. "They say we are twins, but not identical."

The dark-haired girl continued, "Except for

our hair and our height, we do look a lot alike just as any sisters might. I'm Jennifer, and this is Jean." she finished, pointing first to herself then to her sister.

"I'm Rebecca," said Rebecca, "And I'm so glad you are here. It is going to be wonderful having two friends right next door!"

As the women continued to introduce themselves and get acquainted, Daniel and Charles gathered the luggage and started moving toward the wagon. "I wish we had something with a smoother ride than this old wagon," he said apologetically, "This is what we drove to the territory and it is all we have."

Mrs. Cunningham smiled warmly, "I am sure I will be just fine. After that train, I think I am ready for most anything!"

Daniel and Charles studied the wagon, deciding what was the best way for Mrs. Cunningham to make this last leg of her long, tiring journey. Finally, they carefully lifted her from the wheelchair and helped her to sit on the wagon seat. Then they put the chair into the wagon bed and secured it firmly in place. When they moved her back into the chair, she was able to sit with reasonable comfort and safety. After she was in place, they started the trip back to their farms, driving very carefully to avoid the worst of the wagon ruts.

"Oh," said Daniel, pulling the horses to a halt. "I almost forgot. There is a letter for you in the depot. I didn't pick it up because you will probably have to sign for it."

Charles, with a puzzled look, jumped down and hurried into the depot. Soon he returned with the letter in his hand. "There was no place to sign. I guess the postmaster is trusting our honesty!" Charles began to tear into the letter, "I can't imagine who could be sending me a letter." He read it rapidly and his mouth dropped open. He turned to the others with a look of amazement. "My claim to my land is being challenged!" He said unbelievingly, "Someone claims he staked my claim before I did!"

# Chapter 11

## Bad News

The mood during the ride home was somewhat subdued.  Jennifer and Jean looked at each other while fighting to hold back their tears. Rebecca watched Charles as he read the letter again more slowly. He folded it carefully and replaced it in the envelope.

Finally, Jennifer asked, "What does that letter mean, Charles? Do we not have a home after all?"

Jean chimed in, "Will we have to go back to Kansas?"

Rebecca asked in a shaky voice, "What will you do now? Surely you won't have to leave!"

"Well," said Charles, "I know that during the last few weeks, I have walked over every inch of our land. So, I am sure that there was no sign anywhere of anyone else putting in a stake! That is our land! I claimed it fair and square! So, what I will do is the same as I would have done before this letter came." He turned to the three Simpsons and nodded to Daniel, "I will continue working with our other good neighbors, clearing and planting as all of you teach me how. I will report as ordered for the hearing, but in the meantime, we will not worry about it."

"That's my boy!" put in Mrs. Cunningham, her voice quavering a bit.

Daniel placed a hand on Charles' shoulder and said, "You are exactly right not to get too excited yet. They say that there are some people randomly challenging claims with no real grounds at all, hoping they might scare somebody into just giving up a good claim, and then they can grab it."

"I don't know how they will go about deciding this," said Rachel, "But you can be sure we and all our other neighbors will tell them the same thing you have said. There was not anyone else anywhere near that claim on the day of the run, but you!"

"I'm sure it will come out okay," said Charles, "God was so good letting me meet you and my other good neighbors and letting me find such a perfect claim, I feel sure that He is going to see me through this too."

As they arrived back at the claims in the falling dusk, Rachel said, "It's long past suppertime! Everyone must be famished! Won't you share our supper with us? I left a stew cooking in the Dutch oven in the coals, so everything will be ready in a few minutes." She looked at the three girls who were enjoying getting acquainted and added, "Especially with three girls to help with getting everything done!"

When all was ready, Daniel asked a blessing on the food and added a special thanks for bringing Charles' family safely to Norman. In spite of the worry that now loomed over the group, they enjoyed the food, and the conversation was cheerful as they all got better acquainted.

Over the dishwashing and clean-up, the women chattered like they had known each other for years. Mrs. Cunningham revealed that her name was Lucille, and soon it was just Rebecca, Lucille, Jennifer, Jean, and Rachel, good friends and next-door neighbors. Lucille and her girls enthusiastically admired the way the Simpsons had whitewashed the walls, put braided rugs on the floors and curtains at the windows, to decorate their sod house.

"They are so easy to do," said Rachel. "Rebecca and I can teach you some more touches for your new home in no time if you would like."

As the group made happy plans for the future and dark covered the land, it was a tired, but contented, group that parted to go to their own homes to sleep and prepare themselves for a day of hard work tomorrow.

****

In the weeks that followed, the work continued on the new farms. The garden plots that had been prepared earlier had been turned into five gardens with plenty of beans, cabbage, tomatoes, beets, and potatoes planted. Some of the women had used a carefully guarded stash of special seeds of personal favorites like okra, spinach, lettuce, and sweet peas. The men planned to dig cellars soon so that much of the bounty could be canned and stored for the weeks and months ahead. For now, though, the weather was still hot every day and stayed very dry. Buckets of water had to be painstakingly carried from the barrels to the plants that were now flourishing in the gardens.

As the children made their daily watering rounds, they were careful to pull out any weed that dared to show itself. The families worried that the wells in town might go dry if the hot, dry weather continued. Each day they prayed to see some clouds in the sky to bring wonderful, replenishing water to the dry ground and fill the waiting rain barrels. They dreamed of the time when they could have their own wells to supply the water for the neighborhood. The conclusion was always that they must have enough crops this year to afford to have the well dug.

The men had had lengthy discussions about what crops would have the best chance to survive if the hot, dry weather continued.

Robert Bridges had found that his farm had a small pond on it and bought a few milk cows. With a water supply and plentiful prairie grass, they were now supplying milk for his own family and his neighbors. He had planted part of his field with hay in order to have feed for them after the fields of prairie grass had become crop fields.

Daniel had decided he would have a try at cotton, although it was a little late for planting it, and he would have to go to Purcell to sell it. The experienced farmers agreed that it was far too late to put in wheat or oats this year, but they could have another field prepared in plenty of time for next year. Charles decided to follow Daniel's lead and plant cotton. Harvey Miller and Samuel Groggins would both plant corn.

****

As the farms took shape, the little town of Norman was flourishing, and the new settlers were feeling the need for places to worship each week. The different denominations each began to work toward providing a building for their congregations. The South Methodist men had agreed to work together to enlarge and remodel the little building that was on the lot the group had claimed. They had decided that the house could be transformed into a place of worship, quicker and with less expense than tearing it down and starting over. With a steeple and some remodeling inside, it could become an acceptable house of worship. So, each Saturday the men worked together diligently to get the church ready.

During this time, representatives came from both the north and south Methodist churches to organize two churches in the new town. The Rev. J. L. Burrow came to meet with the people who were declaring their intention to be a part of the south Methodists' congregation, and about a month later, the Rev. E. F. Hill came to organize the north Methodists. Rev. Burrow was a busy man organizing the new churches in the territory and had just completed organizing the church in Oklahoma City a short time before coming to Norman. The tasks of the two ministers were to explain the organization and doctrines of their churches to the settlers and help them choose suitable lay-leaders. They would then request that a minister be assigned to the congregation. The south church was organized with 30 members. It would have a Board of Trustees, and a Board of Stewards. Daniel was asked to serve on the Board of Trustees, and other new congregation members filled the remaining positions. With their organization complete, the Rev. A. N. Averyt was appointed to be their pastor and arrived soon to an enthusiastic welcome. The North church did not receive a minister until several months later.

The members of the south church were so eager to have a church that they met in the building each Sunday even while the work was going on. They sat on the floor or on stacks of lumber, or they simply stood while they sang joyful songs of praise for this place God had provided for them. Finally, in July, the work was finished, and the congregation held their first service in their completed sanctuary.

One morning in the following week, Daniel came home from town carrying a newspaper. "Wait till you see this," he called to Rachel who was working inside their sod house. She quickly came out to see what his excitement was about.

"I bought a copy of a newspaper called the *Oklahoma City Journal*," he said waving the paper in his hand. "Listen to this article, 'Norman claims the honor of building the first Protestant church in Oklahoma. Oklahoma City will gracefully take second place in church building and allow Norman the palm.' That first church is the little building our south Methodists have just completed remodeling." He turned to Rachel with a smile as he spread out the paper.

"Well isn't that something!" Rachel mused as she read the article for herself. "Of course, I guess it helped that we had a little building there to start with. It also helped a lot that we had a group who were so eager to have a place to worship!"

Rebecca was listening to the conversation and crowded in to see the paper too. "I sure loved our service yesterday in our new church. All the songs sounded so good, and Pastor Averyt's sermon was so easy to understand. As he said, I guess we really are a little like the Children of Israel making homes in a new land!"

**\*\*\*\***

Life on the five neighboring farms settled into a pleasant system of shared work in the fields for the men and shared work with the gardens and food preserving for the women. As July and August approached, a routine developed for all the families. After a good breakfast and a hot morning of work, they broke for lunch. Afterward, they would take a time of rest during the hot hours of the afternoon. Long hours of daylight allowed them to get in a few more hours of work after the worst of the heat, coming in at dusk to enjoy a light dinner and a pleasant evening of relaxation.

During the afternoon rest periods, Rebecca, Jennifer, and Jean fell into the practice of spreading a quilt in the shade on the east side of one of their little soddies, and there they would while away the rest hours.

As an only child, Rebecca had sometimes yearned for the closeness of a sibling or a good friend. Now she felt her wishes were coming true. Daily, the three girls became closer and closer. They talked of their lives before coming to the territory.

Jennifer and Jean shared the devastation felt by their whole family after their father had died and Charles had tried to run a failing farm alone. Rebecca couldn't help but cry with them as they relived that time. Rebecca felt that her life had been easy by comparison. She had sorrowed for days after her family departed from their home in Missouri, the only home she had ever known in her young life, but that could not compare to the heartbreak of losing a parent and watching another whose health was wasting away.

As will naturally develop in long heart to heart discussions among three girls, the subject of their future here in this new home along with their dreams for their adult lives came up often. Being on the verge of young womanhood they realized that decisions would be required of them soon. Just meeting the necessities of their lives thus far had produced in Jennifer and Jean a maturity beyond their years. Now as they enjoyed time with their newly gained "sister" they enjoyed, for the first time they could remember, a time of just being young women together sharing their secrets.

One day as they lounged on the quilt munching apples, their discussion turned to serious matters, Jennifer said with an air of finality, "Well, I know what is in my future." When the others looked surprised, she continued, "I will never marry. Mother and Charles will always need someone here to care for them."

When the others gasped and began to protest, she continued, "No, let me finish. It just makes sense. Here I am a big, tall gangly girl! No one would ever want to marry me anyway! Now Jean is so petite and cute she is already attracting the boys around her! She will have men waiting in line to ask for her hand."

"No!" Jean sat up with an angry look, "I've

thought about this too! I can't let you give up your freedom to make a life so I can just go merrily on with mine! Even though Mother seems better right now, we all know she is never going to be able to keep the house and do the things she used to do. I don't even want to think of it, but if something happened to her we would still need to take care of Charles. How could he farm this land and take care of a house too? We are both needed here where we are. I don't think we either one can plan on marriage any time in our near future."

An air of quiet contemplation had settled on the small group, so Jennifer shook her head and smiled brightly, "Well, that is enough of that for now. Rebecca, you haven't told us about your dreams."

"Well," said Rebecca thoughtfully "With no brothers or sisters, Mama and Papa and I have always been so close that I have never even been able to imagine marrying and leaving them! I guess there could come a time when I will think differently." She closed her eyes in a dreamy look as she continued. "He would have to be someone very special. Like a knight of old, and he would treat me like a fine lady of royalty!"

When she saw that the other two were listening raptly, she shook her head somewhat sheepishly and said, "That will never happen though. Knights aren't just hanging around in the Unassigned Lands! And, if they were, they wouldn't be interested in a little unsophisticated country girl. I expect that I will be waiting for a long time!"

Just then, Rachel looked around the corner and called, "Rest time over! We have canning to get done this afternoon."

The three young women got up, folded their quilt and returned to the afternoon's work. Something in the relationship had been changed, however, and there was a new bond of shared confidences that they knew would remain strong throughout their lives.

****

By now, the fierce heat of summer had set in, and the families continued to struggle to keep their crops alive. July turned into August with still the hot sun beating down each day and no clouds in the sky to promise the much-needed rain. If a stray cloud did come over and drop a little rain, it dried up almost before hitting the ground. It seemed like a miracle that the water from the wells in town remained sweet and clear in spite of the constant drawing of water for the needs of all the residents of the town.

Careful carrying of water to the gardens had kept most of the plants alive, and, as the produce began to come in, Marian Miller, Janetta Bridges, Rachel and Rebecca Simpson, and the Cunningham women, Lucille, Jennifer, and Jean, brought their big, heavy canners out and worked together to shell, wash, chop, and otherwise prepare the food in shiny jars. They were meticulously processed in the canners and set out to cool. They would later be divided among the families and put away to enjoy when the cold of winter was upon them. Even Lucille was able to come outside in her wheelchair with a basket on her lap to take part in the work and fellowship.

The little settlement, now known as Norman, was quickly becoming a real town making the "trip to town" a noteworthy event. Along with working hard together to get the land cleared, planted, and turned into prosperous farms, the men usually made a trip once a week into town to the feed or hardware stores to pick up supplies needed for the farm work. The women would make their own trip at another time when they had enough time to consider their purchases carefully as well as visit with the many friends they were making.

Early in May, a provisional government had been established for the town. A mayor, Thomas Waggoner, was elected, and they also had a city marshal, a clerk/recorder, and a city council made up of four men. The establishment of at least a simple government had helped to give the residents of both the town and the surrounding area a sense of security and permanence.

A few tents were still in place along the well-worn, dirt streets, but more and more wooden buildings were beginning to show up. Some businesses had invested a few dollars to purchase "squares" to add to the appearance and air of permanency. The 12' X 12' structures were designed to be used singly or joined together for a larger structure. Some of the more affluent residents were purchasing the squares to use temporarily while building a home.

The months passed by quickly as the Territory matured. Most of the residents were feeling happy with the decisions they had made for the life-changing move that had brought them here. Daily they looked around them, pleased with the progress they were making, but still, even as autumn approached the stifling, dry heat continued.

Daily, the eyes of the settlers kept going back to the hot, hard, blue sky and the question in many hearts was, "When? Oh when, Lord? When will it rain?"

# Chapter 12

## Facing the Challenge

*Hello Dear Emmaline,*
*It is hard to realize that we have been here for almost six months! They have been months full of hard work, but also full of so much fun and*

*satisfaction. I cannot imagine our
lives any other way than just as they
are! We have had long, hot days with
lots of work, but they have also been
full of so much fun with our neighbors
and our new friends at church. Papa
and Charles had enough cotton to
each take a load to Purcell to sell.
They don't get much money for one
load, but now, Mama says it is
wonderful to have even that little
extra to add to our shrinking savings.
Papa bought a very sweet-tempered
cow, and we have named her
Bluebelle. It is wonderful to have
plenty of milk to drink and even to
make cheese and cottage cheese! Now
as the weather turns into fall, the
mornings are cool and crisp and,
already, the countryside is beginning
to show promise of its beautiful colors
to come.*

*One thing remains a worry to
all of us. Last week, our next-door
neighbor, Charles, came over to
share a letter he had received from
the land office in Guthrie. . .*

Charles frowned at the letter in his hands as
he, his sisters and his mother gathered with the
Simpsons at their kitchen table. The group was
hardly recognizable as the same people who had

gathered for a meal here back in June. All were lean from months of hard work and wore beautiful, healthy tans. Even Lucille was looking much more fit than when she first came here. She, also, was tanned, and her wheelchair had now been replaced by a walking cane which she kept by the side of her chair.

"It says," he said slowly as he read, "that I have to report to the land office in Guthrie at 10:00 a.m. on the 29th of October for a hearing on the challenge against my ownership of my farm!"

There was an audible groan from the others in the room as he continued. "It tells me the land agents will be hearing the case and what to bring to support my right to this claim." He folded the letter and replaced it in the envelope. "Well, we knew it was going to happen sometime. I am going to be just as glad to get it done and off our minds," he said.

"But it's not fair!" said Jennifer. "Now you have to spend money again on train fare and lose time from taking care of our new farm."

"I don't want you to have to go," wailed Jean. "I am afraid to be here alone with just us and Mom."

"You don't have to worry about being alone," said Rachel, reaching out a comforting hand to Jean. "That is one reason that we have all our claims here close together, so we have friends nearby."

"Would you like to have some company?" asked Daniel. "I can't say if having someone along to vouch for you would help at this point, but Rachel and Rebecca can arrange to get together with your family to make sure everything is taken care of on both our places here."

"That would be wonderful," said Charles brightening. "It would surely be reassuring to have you along."

"That is decided then," said Rachel with finality. "With the crops already in, the five of us women can handle things just fine." She gave Daniel a smile which said without words, "I'm proud of you for recognizing that Charles might need your moral support!"

When the morning of October 29 arrived, the two men took Charles' wagon and, after saying their goodbyes, started into town to catch the early train north. They boarded the train and settled back for a long trip to Guthrie.

Although they were both preoccupied with worry about the outcome of their trip, they couldn't keep from noticing the amazing differences of the communities the train took them through as opposed to their first trip to Guthrie. Now, after six months, most of the tents had been replaced with more permanent structures and the streets of hard-packed dirt were teeming with wagons and people carrying on the bustling commerce of thriving towns.

Daniel did not try to make conversation, respecting Charles' need for quiet. For himself, he closed his eyes and had a long quiet conversation with God, asking him to be with them and to bring them a good outcome.

After a while, Charles let out a long sigh, and

said, "I can't understand it! Why is this happening? Why, after we have come this far and everything was going so well? I didn't want to worry Mom and the girls any more than necessary, but bad things could happen at this meeting. What could I have done wrong? Did I fill out something wrong on the papers? What if they take my farm?" He closed his eyes and put his face into his hands after the outburst.

Daniel put a comforting hand on his shoulder and shook his head sympathetically. "I can't say that I know how you feel, because I have never experienced anything quite like this, but I can imagine how worried I would be if it had happened to me. I can't do much for you except to keep praying for strength for you. And one other thing, you can count on all your new friends to be standing with you no matter what happens."

"I know that and I appreciate it. Maybe I was getting a little too cocky! I was feeling the most confident that I ever have since Dad died! Everything was going so well!" said Charles as he leaned back and drew a deep calming breath. "I do feel better having you with me. I don't feel so alone. God must intend something good to come from this even though we are not able to see it yet."

Soon the train pulled into the Guthrie station and the two friends stepped down to the platform. They walked the familiar, yet not familiar road over to where the land office stood. As with all the other towns, there was almost nothing recognizable. The land office was still there but now was surrounded by so many new structures they had to be careful to find the right one.

As they approached, Charles stopped Daniel with a hand on his elbow and said, "Do you suppose we might have a prayer together before we go in?"

"Of course," said Daniel. The two stopped where they were and turned their backs to the people walking by. As the two stood, elbow to elbow, Daniel prayed, "Lord, we don't always understand your plan, but you have assured us that you will always be beside us. So, Lord, we trust that whatever happens when we go in here, you are there guiding us and giving us wisdom."

To this, Charles said a hearty, "Amen, and Lord, please don't let me disappoint Mom and the girls."

They turned back to the door and ignored the puzzled looks they received from the few who had noticed their prayer. The door was closed and they could hear voices from inside.

"Well, it is only a little after 9:00. Might as well go see if we can find a cup of coffee," said Daniel, "It's on me if we can find a cafe."

They walked over toward the bustling little town looking for a place serving coffee. Just as in Norman, many of the tents had been replaced by simple wooden structures, or some had already acquired some of the "squares" for their places of business. As they looked over the offerings, they found one tent was selling coffee and fresh doughnuts. They decided to treat themselves to coffee with a doughnut since Rachel had been too busy to make those treats yet.

"Makes me feel a little guilty," said Daniel as he sipped his coffee. "We have come up here on a worrisome errand and, yet, here we are splurging like this. I guarantee that Rachel is just about the best cook around, but this comes a mighty close second!"

Charles was also making short work of the pastry on his plate, "Well," he said, "worry about the outcome of the challenge to my claim doesn't seem to have hurt my appetite any. I guess I have to keep my strength up," he continued with a chuckle.

When they had finished, it was nearing 10:00 and time for them to report back to the land office. So, after Daniel paid for their food, they retraced their steps back to the office. They only had a few minutes to wait before the two agents came to the door and invited them inside.

One of them extended a hand to Charles and said, "You must be Mr. Charles Cunningham."

"Yes, I am," replied Charles, "I don't really understand this at all, and I hope we can clear it up quickly." He turned to Daniel and continued, "This is my friend Daniel Simpson. I was on foot on April 22 going in from Downing's Crossing and he gave me a ride. We chose our claims side by side."

Daniel extended his hand, and the four greeted each other all around.

"Have a seat here," invited the second agent. He continued, "I am John Dill, and this is Cassius Barnes. It is too bad that these disagreements arise and we have to call you away from your work like this."

Mr. Barnes added, "We are hoping that it can be settled quickly. The other party to this challenge has also been contacted, and should be here soon."

"I guess it is your job," said Charles, "but you are right it does take us away from our work. I had to leave my sick mother and my two young sisters alone, and it kind of worries me. If we didn't have good neighbors like the Simpsons, I am not sure I could have left them."

"This plan of land runs to distribute the land has some good points, but it has some bad ones too when it leaves room for disagreements like this that must be settled," said Mr. Dill as he sat down behind his desk. "I hope that the government will work on it some before the next time there is land to distribute."

"You are so right there!" said Daniel, "It was exciting and historic, but there is too much possibility of people being hurt, and too much uncertainty about the right solution in these disputes. I can tell you for sure though, that Charles did everything the way it should have been. He was even willing to do it on foot until I came along and took him with us!"

Right then, the door opened, and two more men walked in. They both had carefully trimmed and combed hair and beards. Their clothes were neat and their boots shiny. "Come on," said one of them, "Let's get this going and throw those claim-jumpers off my land!"

"Yeah," said the other, "We shouldn't have to take our good time to come here to correct someone else's mistakes."

The two agents exchanged a quick glance with raised eyebrows, "We do appreciate your taking time out from your work to clean up and come here. Our intention is to handle this as quickly and as fairly as possible. If you will just be seated, we can get started," said Mr. Dill.

"Which one of you is Mr. Reed?" asked Mr. Barnes.

"That's me, Jim Reed," said the man who had spoken first, "This here is Bart Hopkins. He was with me when we saw this guy pull up my stake and throw it away!"

Charles almost jumped out of his seat, "What! That is absolutely not true! There was no stake on my land, and no sign anywhere of any other claim when I placed my stake. I certainly didn't pull one up and throw it away! We were there so soon after noon it is hard to see how anyone could have been there earlier anyway."

"Take it easy, now." said Mr. Dill. "You need to keep calm, and we will ask the questions of each of you in your turn."

Daniel put a comforting hand on Charles' shoulder encouraging him to settle back into his chair. "Relax, Charles. They have to hear everybody out, and we will get to tell our story."

"Sorry," mumbled Charles, "I shouldn't have jumped in like that."

"Ought to be sorry all right," mumbled Mr. Hopkins with a sideways glance at Reed.

The agents placed stacks of paper on their desks with a pencil in hand, ready to listen and take notes. Mr. Dill adjusted his spectacles and continued, "Mr. Cunningham, I will read to you the statement as made to us by Mr. Reed. 'I had galloped my horse all the way past the railroad tracks on that Monday. I rode a little bit farther on across the tracks, jumped off and drove in my stake. Then I went over to rest under a big oak tree and watch the rest of the show. After a while, this guy came riding up. He jumped off his horse, pulled up my stake and threw it away. Then he drove his own stake in. By this time other people had come in all around and they started patting him on the back and calling him 'neighbor.' That is your statement as you gave it to us, Mr. Reed. Do you still state that that is exactly what happened?

Mr. Reed leaned back in his chair and stretched his legs out in front of himself. "That's how it happened, so I sure don't see any reason to change anything," he said smugly.

Mr. Hopkins nodded his head vigorously, "That's the way it was! I was riding along a little bit behind him and saw it all just like that."

"Mr. Hopkins, we haven't asked for a statement from you at this time," put in Mr. Barnes with a stern glare at the two men.

"Well, why haven't you asked?" asked Mr. Reed. "Why don't you get busy and get this done?"

Both Daniel's and Charles' mouths had dropped open in disbelief as this scene unfolded, and they looked at each other in wonder, then at the agents and shook their heads.

"Mr. Reed, if you cannot let me conduct this

interview, I shall have to put you out of my office
and deny your claim!" said Mr. Dill with anger
beginning to tinge his voice.

As the two challengers settled back into their
chairs still grumbling in low voices, Mr. Barnes
turned to Charles and said, "Mr. Cunningham, would
you please tell us your version of what happened on
April 22?"

"I will be glad to," said Charles sitting
forward in his chair. "Well, I had gone to Downing's
crossing since several people had told me that was
one of the places that was very close to some good
claims not far from the boundary. You see, I couldn't
afford a horse as I had to leave my mother and sisters
in Arkansas City with enough money to have a place
to stay and food to eat."

"Come on," Mr. Reed interrupted loudly.
"Get on with it! What does this have to do with him
jumping my claim?"

"Mr. Reed, you have been warned. We would
prefer that we not have to eject you from the room,
but if you make it necessary, we will not hesitate to
continue without you, " said Mr. Barnes in
frustration. "Please continue Mr. Cunningham."

Charles shook his head in wonder and said,
"So there I was right at twelve o'clock noon. I had
nothing but my stake and I was walking toward the
river. I sure wasn't looking forward to crossing it on
foot, but Daniel came along beside me and stopped
to offer me a ride across. And then he let me stay in
their wagon with them! He's a wonderful man, Mr.
Barnes and Mr. Dill. You will never find a better

one. Anyway, they were traveling with five other families, two of them planning to head south at the tracks to go to where the town of Norman was planned to be. Daniel and the other three families continued about a mile east of the tracks, and pretty soon he jumped down to check the soil. He looked at the friends with him, nodded his head, and pounded in his stake. So, I just, stepped across the marked boundary to the next claim and, real quick, I pounded in my own stake. I figured no matter what, I would be sure to have good neighbors. There sure wasn't anyone on either of our claims anywhere in sight!" said Charles emphatically, "As for Mr. Reed and Mr. Hopkins, I've never seen either of them before."

"Do you have anything to add, Mr. Simpson?" asked Mr. Dill.

"Not really," said Daniel, "That pretty well sums it up. I figured he might as well ride with us since there were only me, my wife, and daughter in our wagon. I was pretty sure he wouldn't slow us down any since he doesn't weigh much anyway," said Daniel with a grin at Charles. "What I am wondering though, is whether they are talking about the same place we are. I don't know where he found a big oak tree to rest under since most of what we have around us is prairie grass and little stunted trees."

Mr. Dill and Mr. Barnes both looked questioningly at the two challengers who were squirming angrily in their chairs, having great difficulty keeping quiet.

The agents looked to each other, finished their notes and closed their notepads. "Well gentlemen, do any of you have anything to add?" asked Mr. Barnes.

"Do you mean that's all you're going to do? They're telling you a pack of lies about the whole thing!" fumed Mr. Hopkins. "It's obvious! Everyone was in such a hurry that day, no one would have stopped to pick up a walker! And who cares about how big the tree was?"

"Gentlemen, we are interested in the facts about this challenge, not just more opinions about the other parties' statements." Both agents stood with an air of finality as Mr. Dill spoke. "So, if you have no more facts to add, we will close this interview, as we have other people waiting for us to hear their cases."

"Your statements will be investigated as quickly as possible, and when a decision has been made, you will be contacted," said Mr. Barnes, starting to move toward the door where several more men were waiting outside.

Daniel and Charles stood outside the office while trying to decide what to do next. They were surprised to find out that not quite an hour had passed, for it had seemed like an eternity in that office.

"Better start getting ready to move out, Claim-Jumper!" sneered Mr. Reed as he and Mr. Hopkins followed them out.

"There's no way that anyone is going to believe your lame story! If you are lucky there will still be a few claims left after they give me this one. Of course, they might have a few rocks and trees to deal with," Mr. Hopkins clapped Charles' shoulder as the two challengers swaggered off toward the town.

"Let's go see if we can find something to drink," said Mr. Reed. The sound of their raucous laughter drifted back to Daniel and Charles as they left.

Charles glared at the backs of the pair as he reached around to dust off his shoulder where Hopkins had touched him.

Daniel watched the pair disappear toward town. "There is something about that pair," he said frowning, "It seems like there's something I should know or remember."

Shaking his head, Daniel turned to Charles and said, "If we hurry over to the station, we can still get a train home this morning."

"Sounds good to me," agreed Charles, and the two moved quickly in that direction.

# Chapter 13

## Real Houses

*Hello Dear Emmaline,*
*    Life is moving right along in*
*our fine little town! There is still that*
*dark cloud hanging over us here in*
*our little community of five families.*

*There is still the worry that the Cunningham family might lose their claim and no longer be our neighbors. When Charles and Papa told us about what had happened in Guthrie, we were amazed! How could anyone believe what those terrible men said, even for a minute? Once Charles and Papa got home and told their story, though, they settled right down to work on the farms. They seem to be the least bothered of us all!*

*More and more real houses are appearing in town, replacing many of the sod buildings and tents. Here in our little community, Papa and the other four families have bought the lumber to begin building houses. Although the crops were not very good this year, Papa and the neighbors managed to make deals with the lumber company for the materials for our houses. Our homes will be smaller than we hoped, but the frameworks are now going up for all five houses. With the homes being so small, and all the neighbors working together, the work goes so fast!*

*Another wonderful thing that has happened is that we have our own water! All our neighbors agreed to*

*combine their money and hire a
company in town to come dig three
wells along the shared borders of all
our claims. We can have plenty of
water for the land and cattle, as well
as all the fresh clean water we need
for the house. No more long trips to
haul it from town!*

*I still worry, though, that the
Cunninghams may be putting all this
money and work into their farm and
then lose it to that awful man!*

*Other things are happening in
our little neighborhood! The Millers
are expecting a little baby early next
year! Our friends from in town, the
Carpenters and the Harrises, are also
expecting new babies! They are all so
excited at the idea of starting new
lives in this new territory with new
babies!*

*I am forgetting my own
exciting news! There is going to be a
school and I will be going! A teacher,
Mrs. Mattie Dollarhide will be
holding school soon in our church! It
will cost a little for me to go, but
Papa says that it is worth the cost
because education is very important,
for girls as well as boys!* ...

The year had brought about much progress in

the town and neighboring farms. In August, a bank had opened for business in Norman. It was a branch of a bank in Newton, Kansas which also opened branches in Guthrie, Stillwater, and El Reno. While the bank was an asset to the community, they were not prepared to make loans to individual farmers with their only collateral being the hope for better weather and crops the next year. The homes they intended to build would be of value in time, but not soon enough to secure the loan. The five families had each made some small profits from this first summer of work in spite of the drought. The farmers' only hope to purchase lumber for homes, farm equipment, livestock, and seeds was to make deals with the merchants and write promissory notes for the coming year's profits. They all agreed to limit themselves to the basic necessities for farm life now, continuing to share plows, and other implements.

While the families had all been willing to give up added niceties, they felt that having their own well and water source was a necessity. So, when they had learned that there were some companies in town in the business of digging home and farm wells. The arrangements were made and all the families waited eagerly for the completion of their wells. What a celebration when they had filled the first barrels from their own wells.

Piles of lumber lay stacked and ready on each of the farms where each family had decided to locate their house. The men worked together each day with the goal of completing five simple, one-room homes during this off-season and before the winter weather hit.

As the month of October neared its end in the territory, there was a nip in the morning air. They were already finding out, though, that the weather here was not predictable. While they might have frost in the morning, the afternoon could bring beautiful sunshine and mild temperatures. Many of the days brought almost summer like temperatures. There were some days of the much-needed rain they had looked for all summer, replenishing the dry ground and fields after the crops were already harvested and the fields were in waiting for next year.

Meanwhile, the territory was putting on a show that was nothing short of sensational! The plant-life of the area ranged through the whole palette of colors from pale yellows to the most vivid oranges and reds. Each morning as the sun climbed high in the sky, there seemed to be a whole new world of wonders to see.

In the midst of these wonders, the Simpson family sat around the fire finishing their breakfast hotcakes along with mugs of hot coffee and tea. The exciting subject of discussion was the school that would be opening soon in the town of Norman.

"Mrs. Dollarhide is accepting enrollments starting on the second of November," said Daniel. "It is to be a subscription school, so it will cost us $2.50 for the first term of three months of schooling for Rebecca. We must afford it though. It will be important that her education is up to par, especially here in this new territory with so much to be accomplished. Educated women are going to be very important as things develop."

Rachel refilled her cup and Daniel's from the big, black coffee pot; she poured tea in Rebecca's cup. "Yes," she said thoughtfully, "No one knows what this territory will demand of us, so we need to be prepared. In one or two more terms, Rebecca, you should be able to take your eighth-grade exams. Then in a few more years, you could teach if you wanted to!"

"I wish that Jennifer and Jean would be going with me," said Rebecca wistfully. "It would be so much more fun to go to school with them! I know they finished their eighth-grade exams before leaving West Virginia, but I still wish they were going to be in school too."

"You will be taking little Anna Mae Groggins with you though," reminded her mother, "and you have met several girls and boys your age at church who will be in school with you.!"

Daniel scratched his chin thoughtfully. "Sam Groggins and I have agreed that one of us will take our wagon in each day and come back for you at the end of the day. You are a quick learner, so you should be ready to pass your exams in the spring next year."

Rebecca's eyes shifted to the framework of a house that was rising a little to the west of their camp. "By that time, we will have a real house to live in. I can hardly wait!"

"Oh! Just to have a real house again," said Rachel, her eyes shining. "It's going to be small to

begin with, but we can add on later. Just to have my
stove set up and a room to cook in and places to
sleep seems like an unimaginable luxury! Our dear
little soddie has been wonderful, but I am looking
forward to a real house!"

"We are able to put in most of our time on
the houses now. If the weather holds out, you will
have all those things you are wanting before winter,"
said Daniel, gazing thoughtfully at the framework
beside them.

Rebecca looked over at the Cunninghams'
farm next to theirs, "I pray that Charles and his
family won't put in all their work and money and
then lose it to those awful men!"

"Charles' faith is strong that God has His
hand in this. Worrying won't change anything," said
Daniel. "He is a most extraordinary young man, and
we are blessed to have him for our neighbor!"

****

As one autumn day followed another, the
small houses took shape quickly. The five men
worked nearly all the daylight hours, six days each
week, taking time out only for meals. In spite of the
feeling of urgency, the meals they shared became
like community picnics with good food and fun
during the gorgeous days of autumn. No work was
done on Sundays as they were all agreed that, above
all, the Sabbath day was to be kept for worship and
rest.

It was surprising how little time it took for a

group of five eager men to put up a one-room house. As soon as the roof was on and the doors and windows were all securely in place, the women would work on the inside, as they had on the soddies, plastering, painting, and papering the walls, finishing the floors, and preparing the kitchens for the treasured stoves they had brought with them or were purchasing.

Some were already using their stoves in the soddies they had built, but Rachel was holding out to have her stove installed in her new house! They and some of their neighbors had built tables, chairs, and other pieces of furniture that they were using in their soddies while they waited.

Charles, of course, had not been able to transport anything from his family's old home. So, it was an exciting event on a Saturday morning when he carefully bundled his mother, Lucille, up in blankets and placed her in the wagon. Then he called the girls to come and climb in. They soon arrived at their destination, the Carpenter's general store. The two girls were barely able to contain their excitement as they arrived at the store. The tents had now been replaced by a small building containing two rooms filled with merchandise. Hearing the sounds in the store, the Carpenters' hurried in from their living quarters behind the sales room to greet them enthusiastically.

"Charles, how good it is to see you," said Charlotte, hugging everyone in the group. "I think I can guess why you are here."

James followed Charlotte in, shaking hands

with Charles and greeting all the others. "We have received a pretty big package here for you. I hope you have lots of room in that wagon!" he said laughing.

"That's what we came for," replied Charles. "I am pretty sure we will be able to make room for it."

"I don't mind being a little crowded so we can get our new stove home and into our kitchen," said Jennifer.

"Quick, let's go see it," put in Jean bouncing around with delight.

James and Charles went to the back of the store, and with much puffing and straining, brought out a polished black cast iron stove. They set it down at the front of the store in order for everybody to admire and exclaim about it.

"Look at all the cooking space, and this oven is big enough for at least three pies at a time!" exclaimed Jean.

"And a place here for water, so we always have a supply of hot water!" added Jennifer.

"These girls probably won't be so excited about it after they cook meals on it for a few weeks," said Lucille with a smile.

"You mustn't dash in and right off again. I have some hot coffee and tea back in my kitchen," offered Charlotte. "You must come and sit down to visit a while."

It didn't take much coaxing as they were all eager to share news from their community and hear the news from town to take back to their neighbors.

"That sounds mighty good," said James. "Why don't you ladies go on into the back, and we'll come as soon as we get this loaded in the wagon."

After the women were all settled with cups of coffee or tea, Charlotte said with a smile, "I do have some news we want you to take back to all our friends. We are expecting a baby early next year."

After they expressed excited congratulations, Charlotte continued with the news that their friends the Harrises were expecting a baby also. Lucille shared the news from their little community that young Harvey and Marian Miller would also have a baby soon.

"This is a good place," continued Lucille, "A good place to raise families and make a good life. I am so thankful that I got here while I still have a little time left."

"Of course, you do!" exclaimed Charlotte, "Your health is sure to improve here with the fresh clean air to breathe and so much outdoor activity."

After the visit was finished, Charles lifted his mother back into the wagon, and everyone else scrambled in. It was true that the beautiful new stove took up much of the space now, but all were willing to forgo a little space thinking of how wonderful it would be to have that stove in their little soddie kitchen until their new cabin was finished.

When they arrived back at the farm, the neighbors gathered to help unload and install the wonderful new stove. The women gathered to ooh and aah while touching its smooth surface.

"I can hardly wait to get mine," said Marian

Miller. "It is ordered and should be here soon. I never imagined I would be so eager to get into the kitchen and at the stove!"

The other women nodded and laughed knowingly.

When the excitement was over and neighbors began to move back toward their own homes, Charles took his exhausted mother back to their soddie and made sure she was comfortable before returning to the work on the cabins.

Daniel pulled Charles aside for a moment. "Thought you should know," he said quietly, "You had a visitor while you were gone."

"Who would come to visit me?" said Charles with a puzzled look.

Daniel continued, "Well, he said he was a lawyer. Said you might be interested in his services."

"What?" Charles exploded. "Even if I had money to spare, what would I want with a lawyer?"

"He wouldn't say much. Only that he would return when you were at home and that he was sure he had an offer that might interest you," said Daniel, raising his eyebrows.

"Well, that beats all I ever heard!" said an exasperated Charles. "He didn't say anything besides that? Not when he expected to be back?"

"No," continued Daniel, "I hesitate to even say this, but I had a bit of a feeling about the man. Like I should remember something."

"Don't mention this to Mom or the girls. I don't want them to worry any more than they already are." said Charles resignedly. "I sure hope he comes back soon."

Daniel nodded in agreement with Charles and said, "Keep remembering that God has you right in His hand. He took care of you to get you this far, and He will continue to care for you. You are still in all our prayers!"

The two men parted company and walked silently back to their homes in this land of promise which they were loving more and more with every passing day.

# Chapter 14

## Could This be the Help We Need

At mid-morning the next day work was proceeding on the Simpson's house. Sam Groggins had taken Rebecca and his own daughter Anna Mae to town to Mrs. Dollarhide's school that was now meeting regularly at the Methodist Episcopal Church, South. When he returned, work was already well underway. Some of the men were putting up the frames for the walls, while others cut boards to size to cover the frames. There was a chill in the night air now, so the window frames that would be transferred from the soddies would not be moved until the last. The families would each still have a cozy little home even while they made the move into the new one. In spite of the hint of fall in the air, the men stopped to wipe their foreheads on shirtsleeves frequently as they perspired freely.

Daniel noticed a horse and buggy coming at a fast clip along the road. He went to Charles quietly. "It looks like you have a visitor coming there," he said, motioning toward the approaching vehicle. "That looks about like the rig he was driving yesterday."

Charles wiped his hands and face as he went out to meet the visitor. He walked up to the buggy as it stopped. "I am Charles Cunningham. I understand you were here looking for me yesterday while I was away."

The man, who was wearing a neat gray suit and matching derby hat, jumped down from the buggy. He held out his hand as he approached Charles. "Ah yes, Mr. Cunningham, I understand you are having some problems that I may be able to help with."

Charles backed away from him and said suspiciously, "How did you learn anything about any of my problems?"

"Ah," the man replied, "Certain things in our country are a matter of public record. My name is

Alexander Foster, attorney, and if we can find a place a little quieter away from all this construction, perhaps I can explain why I am here."

"I am going to talk to this gentleman a little while," Charles called to the other workers. "I will be back in a few minutes."

They all nodded and waved him off as he took Mr. Foster over to his own farm to sit in a sunny spot beside the bare framework for his house. "Now, let's hear what you have on your mind, I can't leave my friends doing my work for very long."

Mr. Foster opened a briefcase he had taken from the buggy and took out a handful of papers. "I understand that your claim to this beautiful property is being challenged, and I am here to offer you some help."

"Wait a minute," Charles jumped up angrily, "What business of yours is that?"

"Well, I am a lawyer, and my business is to help people who are being challenged legally. Since my knowledge of the law is rather extensive, I can often help them in ways they aren't able to help themselves." He paused briefly before adding, "For a small fee of course."

Charles laughed grimly, "Well, you've been misled, Mr. Foster. I may have some troubles, but I sure don't have money for any lawyer. Guess you might as well go on your way. There's no business here for you."

"But you see, Mr. Cunningham, there doesn't have to be any money involved. You have a way to pay me right here," Foster said as he motioned out toward Charles' partially cleared farm surrounding them. "You see, all you would need to do to secure my help would be to deed to me a few acres of this beautiful land. I would later sell it for my fee."

Charles looked at him skeptically as he said, "That doesn't even sound legal. It's not my land unless I win against this challenge."

"Ah, that is just it," continued Mr. Foster, "I am the one taking the chance. If we lose your case, I get nothing."

"I'm not sure about that." Charles rubbed his chin thoughtfully, pondering over the idea. "I need to call over a friend for his opinion. He's a lot more experienced in this sort of thing than I am."

With that, Charles walked away without waiting for a reply. He approached Daniel and said quietly, "I don't know about this guy. I don't like him much, but he has a kind of interesting idea. I need another opinion if you can spare a minute."

"Be right back," said Daniel to the other workers as he turned to go with Charles.

Daniel studied Mr. Foster carefully as they approached. He frowned and scratched his head as if trying to stimulate his memory. They shook hands as Daniel said, "I see you did make it back to talk to Mr. Cunningham. He says your idea is sort of interesting."

"Ah, yes," replied Foster, "I think I can be a great help to him."

Foster explained his proposal to Daniel as he had to Charles. All the while the man talked, Daniel studied his face. He closed his eyes and concentrated on the voice. It was clear to Charles that Daniel was searching his memory. He looked troubled as if something just out of reach in his mind was bothering him.

Mr. Foster finished his explanation and silence stretched between them. Finally, Daniel said, "I think my advice to Charles would be to take a day to think this over." He looked to Charles with his eyebrows raised questioningly.

Immediately, Charles addressed Mr. Foster, "I will think this over and if you can return about this time tomorrow, I will have an answer for you."

"Well, now, I don't know about that," said Foster, scratching his chin. "There are several more people I am seeing today, and by tomorrow I may have so many cases that I can no longer take you. You would be smart to accept now."

"You heard what he said," put in Daniel, "Tomorrow or not at all. We will look for you tomorrow." He turned away and returned to the work site.

Charles didn't say any more, just nodded at Mr. Foster as he also returned to work.

"There's just something about him," Daniel said to Charles. "The hat and suit don't seem right. I think he must be a real lawyer. He sure has the language alright. I keep thinking he should be wearing dirty clothes and a slouchy hat. I hope whatever is bothering me comes back to me before tomorrow."

They joined the other men and all worked

steadily until Rachel came out and called to them, "Lunch is ready and waiting for any of these hard workers that are hungry!"

The men hurried to the barrel to wash up and move to where the women had set up lunch on a plank table. As Daniel and Charles brought their plates and sat down side by side, Daniel said, "In my mind I still keep seeing that guy in a dirty plaid shirt, with jeans and boots and a slouchy hat. It seems like he was with a large group of men all wearing about the same." He paused to eat for a while staring off into space. Suddenly he snapped his fingers "That's it! It was at Downing's Crossing. There was a whole gang of rough looking characters hanging around together, and Foster was with them."

Charles, looked at him, "Nothing wrong with that. Even a lawyer won't necessarily be neat and clean all the time."

"But there's more," continued Daniel, "Those other two guys were there! Reed and Hopkins who are trying to take your land! Seems a little coincidental that they would have been together that day, and that Foster would then be offering to be your lawyer!"

Charles sat up and looked at Daniel with a puzzled frown, "What could they be up to? What could they gain from it?"

"I don't know enough about these things to have much idea, but one thing I am pretty sure of is that they have some kind of plan to cheat you out of at least part of your farm!" declared Daniel.

The two sat silently for a few more minutes

finishing their meal.

"So, what can we do now?" ventured Charles.

After another long period of quiet, Daniel said, "I am thinking it is going to mean another trip to Guthrie. Those agents seemed to be very fair, just overwhelmed with too many cases to take care of. If those guys are trying to pull something on you, they are probably doing the same thing with some other settlers. Rachel, if he returns tomorrow, just tell him that Charles decided he didn't need a lawyer. I think our friends can spare us a day from the work here, and we need to be on that train to Guthrie just as soon as possible."

# Chapter 15

## Christmas in the Territory

*Dear Emmaline,*

*We are seeing a ray of hope about setting things right here in the territory. Papa and Charles caught the train yesterday for the trip to*

*Guthrie again. They brought back
very hopeful sounding news. Papa
said that the agents were very glad to
hear their story, and said they did
have a few other similar sounding
cases. While they couldn't drop the
challenge based on this one bit of new
information, they did tell them that
they would investigate, and get back
to them just as soon as possible. That
is turning out to be a long time! The
days and weeks go by. Each day we
are thinking there should surely be
some good news, but nothing
happens!*

*I find it hard to imagine
losing the Cunninghams as our
neighbors! It is so much fun to have
the two girls right next door as my
dear friends! And Charles is such a
good friend! He doesn't treat me as if
I were a child! Maybe because he
thinks of me as almost as old as his
sisters. And dear Mrs. Cunningham,
her health continues to be a worry,
but she never complains. We have
heard that there will be a doctor here
in town soon. Dear Lucille certainly
does need one!*

*As I write this today,
Christmas is approaching. It will
certainly be a different one, but I just*

*know that it will be the best one of*
*our lives! ...*

As Daniel and Charles had expected, Mr.
Foster never came back, which seemed to confirm
their suspicions that something illegal had been
going on! How sad it was to think of someone with
his legal training putting it to such misuse! As
before, they put their worries aside and applied
themselves to working with their neighbors to
provide secure dwellings. It was proceeding quickly,
and now, in early December, all of the five families
in the little community had at least shells of one-
room houses on their farms. They were small, and
there was still work to be done finishing the insides,
but they would be comfortable shelters for the
winter.

Rachel stood admiring her new kitchen.
Rays of sunlight shone through the shiny glass
window belying the cold temperature outside. The
cast iron stove that had come with them from
Missouri put out enough heat to keep the room cozy.
As Rachel looked around, she added another prayer
of thanks to the hundreds she had already prayed.
The room was very small, but the fact that there was
very little furniture, made it appear roomier than it
was.

The stove was the star of the room, sitting
regally in its corner. The room also held a small
cabinet base with a worktop and dry sink in it. A
small single cot for Rebecca sat against the wall in
one corner, and a larger one for her parents in the

other corner of the same wall. A folding table with four chairs provided a place where the family could enjoy a meal together and it could be folded compactly against the wall when not in use. Two rough, but comfortably padded easy chairs and a third smaller one completed the furnishings of the room and turned it into a comfortable sitting room in which to enjoy the long winter evenings.

Now she examined the room with the question in mind of where would be the best place for a Christmas tree. Over the past few months, exploration of the area had shown that many of the gullies or streams contained numerous small cedar trees that would serve the purpose nicely. Finally, she settled on the corner farthest away from the stove. *Must keep it from drying out too quickly,* she thought. *What size? Maybe just about Rebecca's height. Yes, we will get Daniel to take us looking for one tomorrow!* With that decided, she began dragging the furniture around to make a clear spot for the tree where they could enjoy it while they sat at the table for meals, or reading in the easy chairs on a long restful evening.

That afternoon when Daniel came in bringing Rebecca home from school, they quickly noticed the difference in the room.

"What's this," asked Daniel looking around, "Did you decide we need a new look to this room already?"

"Now Daniel," Rachel laughed, "Just think for a minute! What time of year is it? Here we are into December already!"

Rebecca twirled around the room with a smile on her face, "I know! I know what Mama's thinking of. It's time to get a Christmas tree!" She looked at her mother with questioning eyes, "Isn't that right, Mama?"

"Yes, I think one just about your height would fit well into this corner right here, and I thought maybe we should go look over the area tomorrow to see if we can find one to cut." Rachel looked to Daniel for his nod.

"Sounds like a good idea to me," said Daniel. "We can hitch the team up early in the morning. We might better plan on taking a lunch along and making a day of it. It may take some time to find a good one since they are a little scattered."

"Oh!" enthused Rebecca, "May I go ask Jennifer and Jean to come along. I know they will want a tree too. And maybe little Anna Mae Groggins would want to come."

"Oh, yes," Rachel's eyes glowed as she began to plan, "Let's tell all the neighbors and make a party out of it! Maybe we can find some bright berries and greenery to use for decorations, and we can make some chains out of colored paper."

"Maybe you could make some of those dough ornaments you color and bake," added Rebecca.

"We may have to search all the gullies and streams in the area to find just the right trees and berries or greenery. Looking at the land, you can tell that there have been wildfires in the past that have kept the small cedars down. I have noticed, though, that some of them in protected or wet places have survived to a pretty good size. Better tell everybody to bring a lunch. It may take a while!" put in Daniel, catching their enthusiasm.

With that, Rebecca hurried off to find Jean and Jennifer and the three of them ran to tell their neighbors of the impromptu party.

Thus, it was that the next morning three wagons filled with warmly dressed, excited people gathered in the field behind the Simpsons' house. The Bridges and Millers had decided to ride together, as had the Simpsons and Cunninghams. The Groggins, with their larger family, took their own wagon. Only Lucille Cunningham stayed behind, having decided it would be wise for her to stay in out of the cold. They began an excited parade circling through the five farms searching the likely spots where small groves of evergreens might be hiding.

They called back and forth between wagons and, as they went along they pointed out likely spots to find greenery. When they came to the dividing line between the Groggins and Bridges farms, they found behind a small embankment a little grove of cedar trees. The women and children clapped their hands with excitement and cries of "Yes," and "These look like good trees," and "These are just right." The wagons pulled to a stop and everyone climbed out. The older children quickly began running through the small grove examining each tree looking for the perfect one.

Rebecca found a pretty, bright green, well-shaped tree and measured it against her height. "Just right! Papa," she called, "Can we take this one?"

Daniel and Rachel came hurrying up. They examined the tree carefully from all sides, then nodded in agreement. Daniel went back to the wagon for his saw. He made short work of cutting, dragging back to the wagon, and loading the little tree. Rebecca then ran to where Jennifer and Jean had just agreed on a tree and gotten Charles' approval.

"Papa!" called Rebecca, "I have an idea! Do you think we could take one for the church? We are supposed to have a Christmas program soon, and wouldn't it be nice to have the church all decorated?" Her parents affirmed the idea and quickly found a second tree.

Meanwhile, each of the other families found just the tree that met their needs. They were also able to cut several nicely colored and shaped boughs of cedar. Careful searching of all five farms revealed several big leafless trees with large bunches of mistletoe clinging to the limbs. When all their finds were loaded, and everyone had as much decorating material as their wagons could hold, it was time to take their lunch break and share the lunches they had brought.

After finishing the lunches and enjoying a time of rest they all climbed back into their wagons and started the trek home. As they drove along, someone in one wagon would start a Christmas carol which was picked up by the others. As soon as that one was finished, another was started. They were having such fun that the time went too quickly as they drove along.

They made short work of unloading and sorting the greenery for each family. There was also a stack that would be taken to the little church in town tomorrow.

While the men set about nailing stands on the bottoms of their trees, the women made hot chocolate and brought cookies or special treats from their homes. Charles went into his house, bundled up his mother in warm quilts and brought her outside to enjoy the festivities. After the hot chocolate and treats had been consumed, the families said their goodbyes and made their way to their own homes where they would carefully decorate the trees.

****

On the following Sunday morning when the congregation arrived at the Methodist Episcopal Church, South, a beautifully decorated cedar tree stood in the front corner of the little church, and greenery was arranged around all the windows and the altar. Some members of the congregation were heard to wonder who had been so thoughtful to prepare the building for the enjoyment of all. The Simpsons, Grogginses, and Cunninghams exchanged knowing glances, but no one offered any suggestions as to who might be responsible. When the Rev. Farris announced a special Christmas Eve Service on the coming Tuesday and suggested that they invite their neighbors and friends, the congregation murmured with delight. There were not many churches meeting in the territory yet, and they knew their friends would welcome a chance to be in church on Christmas Eve.

When the families arrived at home, they hurried to tell the neighbors of the special service and invite them to come whether they were south Methodists or not. Rachel and Rebecca set about preparing small presents that they could take to the service to go under the tree for all the children. Jennifer and Jean hurried home to check on their mother, and to also involve her in preparing gifts.

The neighbors gathered on Tuesday evening to drive into town together. Even Mrs. Cunningham was there, wrapped warmly in quilts. After a joyful drive under a star-filled sky, the group arrived at the church. It was already beginning to fill up, so those who had brought gifts for members of the congregation quickly found places for the presents under the tree. As they looked around, they saw their friends, the Carpenters, were there and the Harrises had also come even though they were Baptists.

The Harrises greeted the group, and Roger said "We are sure glad the south Methodists are having this service and inviting us all to come. Wouldn't seem right not to be in church on Christmas Eve."

As they hurried to find seats, the Simpsons and Cunninghams wound up in the same row, and Rebecca was sitting next to Charles with Mrs. Cunningham, Jennifer, and Jean on his other side. Mrs. Cunningham's face was somewhat pale and tired looking, but she had a glow of happiness as she sat there. As Rebecca glanced up to the side, Charles' face also looked at peace and filled with the joy of the season. She wondered, *How can he put all his problems out of his mind like that? How can he not be worrying about whether he will lose his land or whether his mother's health will improve? Are all adults that way? Will I ever be like that, just able to turn my problems over to God, and then not worry? But Charles is only seventeen now, just a few years older than I am! Does it really make him an adult to be head of his family? If being an adult is really something that happens in your mind, he certainly is that!*

As if sensing her glance, Charles looked at Rebecca, gave her a wink and whispered, "Hope this is just the first one of many, many Christmases right here in our church with you and your family and these wonderful people."

Rebecca nodded her head emphatically in agreement. By this time the building was filled beyond capacity. It seemed that they could barely breathe, but that did not interfere with anyone's good spirits as the service proceeded.

When it was over and the presents had been distributed and opened, nobody seemed to want to leave. It was as though everyone sensed something very special about this occasion, and that there would never be another "First Christmas in the Territory." In spite of the tight space, people circulated through the crowd, managing to greet friends with a "Merry Christmas." It was after midnight when, finally, people made their way to their wagons and buggies and headed toward their homes. Children fell asleep in their parents' arms as the five neighbor families again made their way home under the starry skies.

On Christmas morning after the presents under the tree had been opened, the Cunninghams and Simpsons shared a festive dinner together, while just north of them the Millers, Bridges, and Groggins did the same.

In the evening, a tired and happy Rebecca headed to bed. She found herself filled with a sense of wellbeing and a certainty that they were all in God's hands. She felt an assurance that everything would work out just the way He had planned it.

# Chapter 16

## A Brand New Year

*Hello Emmaline,*
*Here it is 1890! We have just*
*spent the most wonderful Christmas*
*of our lives here in our new home. My*
*gifts were so wonderful! There was a*

*very strange thing about them as not one was a toy! And now that I am thinking about it, that is just the way I wanted it! I think maybe I am too old for toys anymore! When I think back, I have been so busy with all the new things and school I don't even seem to have any interest in my dear doll, Sally! I seldom think to put new clothes on her. I find myself thinking that maybe one day I will have a daughter to give her to. There are so many more things to be done! Mama and Papa gave me beautiful fabric for two new dresses. Mama is going to teach me how to make them! (No wonder I am not interested in doll clothes anymore!) They also gave me a second book for your chest, to use after I have filled up this first one. We made warm gloves for all the Cunninghams, and each of them said we had guessed their favorite colors just right. They gave me a long warm woolen scarf. It feels so warm when this prarie wind comes tearing through.*

*But now Emmaline, it is time to plan for a new year. I will test for my eighth-grade certificate in another month or so and must decide what to do then. Jennifer, Jean and I have*

*spent a lot of time thinking about
that! We would all like to be able to
continue going to school...*

The New Year brought the group of
neighbors together again as they looked back on the
year past and forward to the one to come. The
Simpsons' small home was filled to overflowing
with the congenial group. Altogether 17 people,
including children and babies, were crowded into the
small room. No one seemed to mind the closeness as
each family cheerfully found a small spot to occupy
while Rachel and Rebecca scurried around the stove
and table preparing the simple meal.

Lucille Cunningham occupied one of the
padded chairs with Charles and the girls sitting on
the floor near her. Janetta Bridges sat in one of the
kitchen chairs holding baby Mary Annette while
Robert Bridges stood behind her. Young Harvey and
Marian Miller sat on a quilt near the warmth of the
stove. Samuel and Miranda Groggins had one of the
easy chairs in a corner with a small space around it
where Anna Mae, Mason, and Brewster amused
themselves with a few small toys they had brought
along. Daniel stood by the door, watchful and ready
to offer Rachel a hand with any heavy lifting.

Anna Mae had become a constant shadow to
the three older girls and now kept slipping through
the crowded room to try to involve them in the game
she was playing.

"This is the Mama," she said of the small
carved wooden doll in her hand. She held up another

and said "And this is the Papa. Their babies are already in bed." she told Jennifer, then confided in a low voice, "They have to be in bed now because Papa hasn't carved me enough dolls for the babies yet."

"I am sure the babies will sleep through the night so the Mama and Papa can come to our party," agreed Jennifer with a smile.

"Oh, yes they are very good babies," said Anna Mae, nodding her head solemnly.

Just then, Rachel opened the big oven of her stove and Daniel hurried to grab some hot pads to lift the big pans of cornbread out for her. He placed them on a warm spot on the stove. After Rachel had cut the bread and placed pieces on large platters those were placed on the table which had been opened to its full length. Already on it were other platters and bowls which held desserts, relishes, and salads that had been brought by the guests.

"Ummm," commented Harvey, "Cornbread on New Year's Day means gold or money in the coming year. We can all use some of that!"

"Don't forget the black-eyed peas with ham." put in Rachel as she stirred the big pot on the stove. "These are done now, and I think there are plenty here to bring a big helping of good luck for everybody!"

"If everything is ready, I think it is time to pray," said Daniel. "Then Rachel, Rebecca, and I will bring the food and serve you where you are. I think it might be impossible to move if we all tried to move around to serve ourselves. I hope you're all relatively comfortable and won't mind holding your plate while you eat."

"No long prayers, now Dan," kidded Charles, "That smells too good to concentrate on praying for very long!"

All in the room bowed their heads as Daniel led a prayer of fervent thanks for the loving care they had all received and he then asked for guidance in the year to come.

Rachel spooned the peas and ham quickly into bowls which Daniel delivered to all the guests. Rebecca picked up a platter of cornbread and followed Daniel around to serve each guest. By that time, Daniel and Rachel had finished distributing the bowls of peas and picked up plates of relishes and salads to pass around. After everything was served except dessert, the room became very quiet as everybody began to savor their meals. The only sounds heard were comments of, "U-m-m-m," "Delicious," and "Wonderful." The desserts of sugar cookies and dried-apple cobbler were soon served in a like manner.

After the food was finished, the conversation naturally moved to thoughts of the coming year and what they hoped for in it.

"Well," said Daniel, "I am certainly planning on getting more land cleared and praying for better weather to bring in good crops."

The men all nodded their heads in agreement. "I guess that is what all of us had in mind when we first came to this territory," Harvey said, "But I don't know much we can do to ensure that the weather is good for the crops."

Samuel joined in "That is what farming has always been about. You have some good years, and you have some bad years. Those of us that have farming in our blood, just keep believing that there will be more of the good than the bad."

"Sometimes we are right, and sometimes wrong, but we still stay in there," Daniel said thoughtfully. "We just keep believing that if we give our best, the Lord will give us more of the good than the bad."

"We never know what a year will bring," said Charles. "This time last year, Mom and the girls and I surely didn't think that Dad would die and that we would be here hundreds of miles from what we had thought was our home forever. But now, here we are and it looks like we are looking forward to a great life."

Rebecca watched him as he expressed those deep thoughts and she thought to herself, *How wonderful that God brought all of us together! I can't imagine our lives without Charles. And of course, all of his family!"* She kept her thoughts to herself not feeling quite confident enough to express something so personal here in front of all of their friends.

Thus, the conversation continued as each person there told their hopes for the new year. Finally, as the hour grew later, they made their preparations to leave for their own homes.

"I guess we all meet tomorrow morning out at the Bridges' house to see if we can't get started finishing the inside of it," said Daniel as the neighbors filed out through the door.

After all were gone and the little house was empty again, Rebecca turned to her father with a puzzled look and said, "Did you notice, Papa? Charles didn't even say anything about hoping to see the challenge to his claim settled fairly, and those men brought to justice."

"That's right," he replied. "I think he feels like I do, that God has already guided us to the right solution, and now we just have to realize that it is in His hands and wait for His timing."

"I think," put in Rachel, "that all the Cunninghams know that God has good things in store for them and that they just have to follow His lead each day."

"But I just can't help thinking of all the things I want to see happen. I want to pass my eighth-grade exams, and I want that new school we have heard is coming to be started so that Jennifer, Jean, and I can all go to it. There are just so many exciting things to think about." wailed Rebecca.

"Just think," said Rachel, "in such a short time here in this new place we will already have a college! They have said that they will have courses for anyone who has earned their eighth-grade certificate. It should be just in time for all you girls. I am so glad that the South Methodist church has the foresight to start it here in this new territory."

"Who would have thought a year ago that we would be here looking forward to these exciting things? I guess that's what makes it such a wonderful life," said Daniel smiling. "We never know what good things God has in store for us."

# Chapter 17

## Making a Life

*Dear Emmaline,*
*    Well, Emmaline, 1890 is*
*underway and it doesn't seem much*
*different than 1889! The work of*
*making a home here goes on. Mama,*

*Papa, and I are still working each day to make our home here a little more comfortable.*

*People are still saying that there will soon be a college here in our town! Even more interesting it will be brought here by our church! The Methodist Episcopal Church, South will open a school by the end of the year! I do so hope that it is true. That would be just in time for me to take some more classes past the eighth grade if it is not too expensive! Jennifer and Jean are both hoping that they might be able to go too. I can hardly wait!*

*We had also been hoping every day that there might be some news about the challenge to Charles' claim. Then just today when Charles came back from town, he came hurrying over to share a letter he had just received...*

It was a sunny February day with a reminder of winter still in the air, and the Simpsons were just ready to sit down at the table for lunch when the loud knocking sounded at the door. Rachel went to answer it, and Charles hurried in followed closely by Jennifer and Jean. He was waving a letter excitedly in the air as he called, "Come listen to this. It's from the land office! You won't believe it!"

"Sit down, sit down," said Daniel indicating a chair, "Rebecca, get a cup of coffee for Charles," he continued.

Charles accepted the coffee with thanks and then read "Dear Mr. Cunningham, We are pleased to be able to notify you that the challenge to your claim has been withdrawn and your claim is clear, subject only to the same requirements for improving the land as apply to all claims. We would also like to express our thanks to you and Mr. Simpson for your assistance in uncovering a scheme intended to deprive many of our honest settlers of portions of their rightful claims."

All those in the room cheered and clapped their hands as they exchanged hugs all around. "The letter goes on to describe how this group would pick out young, inexperienced settlers who had gotten a desirable spot." Charles paused with a grim smile, "I guess that describes me, doesn't it?" Then he continued, "The letter says that they would file a challenge against him using some story like they told about mine. Then, while the settler was worried, one of their group with legal training would show up and offer to represent the settler for a portion of their land. The contract wouldn't specify anything the lawyer had to do, just that he would receive a portion of the land if the settler got to keep his claim!

"I see now!" said Daniel. "Then as soon as the agreement was signed, they would go in and drop the challenge, but they would still be able, according to the contract, to receive part of the land!"

"That's right!" said Charles. "There were

185

several different teams working in different areas. To sound convincing, the lawyer had to be someone who actually knew a little law, but they would change who would play the other roles so the same person didn't show up at the land office over and over challenging different claims. Sometimes they would work the same scheme on claims at the other office in Kingfisher, too."

"So, after they acquired a lot of small plots of land, they planned to sell them! They probably planned on first approaching the original settler and offering to sell it back to him," said Daniel thoughtfully.

"That sounds so complicated," said Rebecca. "It looks like it would have been simpler just to do like we did and claim land for themselves."

"But then they would have had to work on the claim. They would have had to make some improvements just like we have done to be able to homestead it," said Daniel.

"What a shame! For someone with training in the law to waste it on such a shameful scheme! It just doesn't make sense," said Rachel shaking her head. "But it surely is a relief to know that it is all settled. Now to other matters. Lunch is ready and on the table. Won't you sit down with us? I always have a lot of extra food cooked. Jennifer, why don't you go over and ask if your mother feels like coming over. Charles and Daniel could go bring her over."

The twins looked at Charles and, when he nodded, they raced out the door.

Charles shook his head as he spoke to the rest

of the group. "I am sure she won't come. Maybe we might take a plate to her. I am just really worried about her. We plan to see one of the new doctors in town soon." He paused, then with a puzzled look, continued, "But, in spite of her health, she is so happy all the time. Says she has never been happier!"

Rachel smiled at Charles, "Yes I have seen that. She just feels so blessed to have had this time here with you, her family, in this place. For a while when you first brought her here, it seemed like the fresh air helped so much and she looked much better. I am afraid, though, that the real cause of her illness is still there. I am eager for you to be able to take her to see a doctor. I know it is hard for you and the girls to watch her health decline this way, but keep in mind that she loves being here and would have it no other way. That may help you a little."

"Thanks," said Charles, "I just have to keep reminding myself."

The girls returned from next door, and as predicted, their news was that Lucille was just too weak to come. The family and friends quickly sat down, gave thanks, and began to pass the food. Neighborly conversation flowed easily around the table.

"Did anyone else talk to the new couple in church on Sunday?" asked Rachel.

"I talked to them for a little while," said Daniel. "It seems their name is McFarlin. He is Robert and she is Ida. Their baby girl is Leta. They came up from Texas to look into cattle raising here in the area. They have acquired a farm just west of town. He is interested in putting a small herd of cattle there."

"I was in the group visiting with him for a little while too," put in Charles. "Everybody kept warning him that, with the dry weather last year, and what seems to be in store for this next year, he better not count on much success with the cattle."

"I heard that," said Rachel. "He went on to say he also plans to start some kind of farming-related business like maybe a feed store."

"I think the man must be a lot like I am," mused Daniel, "Cattle raising is in his blood, just as farming is in mine."

"We must remember to keep that family in our prayers," Rachel put in thoughtfully, "And we might go by to visit soon and see if we can do anything to help them get settled. What do you think Rebecca? You might even get a chance to play with that sweet baby girl."

"Oh yes! I would like that. I could make a cake to take to them," put in Rebecca. "I am getting pretty good at baking chocolate cakes! And, I can hardly wait to play with little Leta."

"That is a good idea; let's plan on that for tomorrow," put in Rachel. "Maybe Jennifer and Jean want to come along."

With Charles' permission, the girls accepted quickly and the three girls put their heads together to plan their trip to welcome the new friends.

When Charles drove his wagon into town the next day Rachel, Rebecca, Jennifer, and Jean were all there chattering away as they anticipated a visit with this new family. Before leaving they had carefully loaded into the wagon a luscious-looking chocolate cake freshly baked by Rebecca that morning, a pot of beef stew, and a pan of cornbread. This would certainly make the McFarlins feel welcome in this town.

# Chapter 18

## A Year of Tears

*Hello Dear Emmaline,*
*Yes, it is I, Rebecca Jane! So*
*much happens and the time goes by so*
*quickly! Norman has come very far,*
*just as our farms have also made so*
*much progress. Our few cleared fields*

*have grown to be real farms with grain in the fields and cattle in the pastures.*

*As 1890 began, we were working hard to build some of the things here that we had all left behind. Especially, we wanted schools, churches, nice houses, stores to shop in, a well filled with clear, clean water, and, yes, we wanted a name! Many of us were wondering when our new homes would officially have a name. Surely, we wouldn't be "the Unassigned Lands" forever! Well, after we had been here for just over a year, the United States Congress took care of it! On May 2, 1890 they made our name The Oklahoma Territory. They say that it is from a Choctaw word that sounds almost like that and it means Red People. Sometimes it had already been called the Oklahoma Lands, but now it is official*

*Now 1894 is nearly over, and our town is growing up. It has become quite civilized. I am growing up right along beside it! And, yes, I have been so busy with all that has happened that I have neglected writing anything in these pages! Still worse, Emmaline, I didn't even know*

*where you were! Today, Mama and I*
*were putting up wallpaper in my*
*room and moving the furniture. There*
*you were, tucked away in the closet!!*
*I have had five birthdays come and go*
*since we came to this territory, and I*
*am now eighteen! Does being an*
*adult make you feel sorrows more*
*deeply? Maybe that is why I have put*
*off this writing. Even now, I fear that,*
*as I write about these years, I may*
*drip tears on your pages. Maybe, as I*
*take my pen in hand, I can lay to rest*
*my sorrowful memories and just*
*remember the happy times. So,*
*Emmaline . . .*

The beautiful box that Rebecca had received so long ago now showed some signs of age. After more than five years, the embossed silver designs on its cover had a bit of tarnish which added a richness to its patina. Age had made it more beautiful and writing in the enclosed books was more of a joy than ever. Some of the events she recorded made her smile while others brought tears to her eyes.

Norman was now a beautiful, busy little town. In the outlying farms one might still see a few soddies, but for the most part, attractive wooden houses had replaced them. The Simpsons, Cunninghams, Millers, Bridges, and Groggins who had come into the territory together and claimed their land to make up a small community of friends, now had attractive wooden homes on their farms. They had all started with one or two rooms when they worked together to put up those first homes. Now rooms had been added as their families and their needs grew. As farmers, none of them expected to make large sums of money, but they did bring in enough to make comfortable, attractive homes and to purchase the equipment needed to work their land. There was a great feeling of satisfaction and contentment in working the farms together and sharing with good neighbors.

In the town of Norman, Main Street had become a thriving little business area with several banks, restaurants, general stores, and other businesses there.

A few blocks to the north of the church and east of the railroad, a neighborhood had grown up that was coming to be known as "Silk Stocking Row" Many of the more affluent families of Norman had chosen to settle there and the houses were a joy to see! When the Simpsons would drive into town, Rebecca often requested that they go down Peters so she could gaze in awe at the beautiful homes there.

Rebecca especially loved to go by during the summer when, through the wide-open windows, the beautiful lace curtains could be seen waving gently in the summer breeze. She would dream about the lives of the refined people who lived within those walls. Sometimes they would be treated to the musical sounds of a piano being played by one of the residents. The notes floating gently through the windows provided a concert for those passing by.

She often said to her mother, "I would love to see the inside of one of those houses, wouldn't you?"

Rachel would reply, "We are blessed with a comfortable home, a loving family, and wonderful, helpful neighbors. What more could we ask?"

It was clear that spiritual life was very important to these early settlers, and no community was complete until their churches were established. Right after the run, an Oklahoma City newspaper had credited the Methodist Episcopal Church, South, in Norman as the first congregation to construct a building in the new territory. Other churches followed rapidly. The north branch of Methodism, the congregation of the First Methodist Episcopal Church, had built diagonally through the block from the south church and dedicated their building in August of 1891. Those of their friends who were north Methodists were now happily attending their own church. Often on Sunday mornings, the members of the congregations would wave at each other across the block. Sometimes the children ran across the distance to engage in a quick game of tag until their parents called them back for the services.

In addition to the north Methodists now sharing their block, the Presbyterian church had been built on the same block just south of them, and other churches were soon going up on other lots in central Norman as the Catholics, Baptists, Episcopalians, and other denominations began to appear. As soon as the churches were built, the congregations filled them to capacity! Both the Methodist Episcopal Church, South and The First Methodist Episcopal

Church increased in membership becoming closely-knit families of believers. As in any community, there were deaths to be mourned and new births and weddings to be celebrated. Being part of a strong faith family helped to get them through the hard times and increased their joy in the good ones.

\*\*\*\*

In 1890, following months of rumors and expectations, the Wesleyan School had come to Norman. It was a small college sponsored by the Methodist Episcopal Church, South. The timing could not have been more perfect for Rebecca, Jennifer, and Jean since Rebecca had just finished the eighth grade, and Jennifer and Jean had also been hoping for a chance to get some more schooling. The Methodist college was to be established in Norman. Since there was no high school in the area the school would offer high school level courses as well as college level. The Rev. J. T. Farris was appointed as head of the school and he worked diligently to be ready to hold classes by September of 1890. Plans were made for classes to meet in the little church of the South Methodists. Norman had just opened a public, tuition-free school in a little building on Dawes built for that purpose. The subscription school that had met in the church for two terms was no longer needed and had closed in May of 1890. Thus, the Methodist Episcopal Church, South building was now available as a temporary meeting place for the new college, which was being called the Wesleyan School. By careful management of their scarce funds, Daniel and Charles both found the money for the $3.00 per month tuition for Rebecca, Jennifer, and Jean. In August, Daniel and Charles took the excited girls to town to enroll in the new college along with as many other young men and women as could be spared from work on family farms. When September came around, they began to attend Wesleyan School classes held in their own little church building. The girls were happy to be a part of the school. At the end of the term, they could hardly wait to see what classes President Farris had planned to be taught the next term. An exciting development in 1891 was the selection and purchase of a site about five blocks to the east and south of their church with plans that the Wesleyan School was to be built there. In the spring of 1892, work began on the building and in June the cornerstone was laid.

In spite of all the hopes and prayers, hot, dry weather had continued to plague the new settlers during these years. Each year they were convinced that this would be the year that would bring sufficient rains for more plentiful crops. Their hopes were not to be realized, however, and as the dry weather continued, many of the ambitious plans of the settlers did not come about. As the hot winds had dried up the crops and plans of the settlers, so the funds dried up for the Wesleyan School and the work was very slow. Prospects for the school were not looking good and President Farris had resigned his position. Finding a new prospect for the position of president of the Wesleyan school proved to be a difficult task. Finally, in 1893 the Rev. A. J. Worley, who was the current minister at the south church, accepted the job. He invested his own money into the building of the school as well as the construction of a residence for women students. The building was finally completed and opened in the fall of 1894 as a school for women.

The Simpson and Cunningham families discussed the situation as they sat around the table one Sunday afternoon. The twins were now 18 years old and much matured by their years of living in the territory. Rebecca at 17 reflected the same increased maturity as her friends.

"It is so hard to know what to plan next year," said Rebecca with a concerned look on her face. "I want to continue at our school, but it seems like it will never get finished!"

Jennifer considered it, "Well, I guess it won't be that bad for us. All three of us are qualified to teach right now."

"Yes," put in Jean, "Eighth grade is all that is required to teach and that is about the only job open to us as women anyway."

"Yes, I know that's true," said Rebecca thoughtfully, "But I also know that I, at least, would be terrified right now to walk into a room full of children to teach a class. Even though I have quite a few classes past eighth grade now, I would want a lot more education before I would try teaching any children!"

"I must say that our church is not offering a

very attractive opportunity at our school for any educator to take this job! I can't imagine what must have convinced Rev. Worley to take the job," said Daniel thoughtfully.

"Imagine the president of the college having to use his own money to keep the school going and to build the girls' residence! He would have to be really dedicated to the school!" said Rachel, shaking her head.

Charles considered all that the others had said and then added, "I don't see how our school will be able to continue here. The territorial university will be offering free classes. Who would pass up free classes to pay fees at our school?"

"I think it is a shame," said Daniel. "I believe our young people need to get their education in the Christian atmosphere of our school. I don't like to make dire predictions, but I am afraid our school won't last long with the university open here."

After many delays, the building was finished at the beginning of fall classes in 1894 and the school moved in. The students were excited to have a new name along with the new building. The Wesleyan School was now the all-female school, "High-Gate College--Gateway to the College City."

Daniel's words, however, proved to be prophetic. The school continued to struggle for another year with not enough students to provide tuition to cover the expenses. By the end of 1894, the school had closed and Rev. Worley had been appointed to a prestigious church in Purcell. The building just completed was sold to the incorporators of a new venture, The Oklahoma Sanitarium Company, which would treat those whose mental stability could not hold up to the many trials of life faced by pioneers.

The territorial university was available, but, since the three girls had all enjoyed four years of work at The Methodist Episcopal college, they and their families decided that they would not pursue any more schooling even though the university was offering tuition-free classes.

****

During this time, the declining health of their dear friend, Lucille Cunningham was a continuing worry in the minds of their neighborhood friends. Lucille dearly loved this territory which had become her home. She seemed much improved for a while, and even regained a little color into her pale features. As time went on, however, her new energy seemed to fade again.

By the mid-1890s, several doctors had come to Norman, and Charles had soon taken his mother to see one of them. When he came home, he had sought out the Simpson family with his news. "The Doctor says it is her heart! He says that there is no hope that it will get any better, but that if we just keep her from too much exertion, we might be able to slow the deterioration," Charles paused with anguish in his face and his voice. Then he continued, "How can I ever tell Jennifer and Jean? Mom didn't even seem bothered when the doctor told us! She says that just getting to come here and live in this wonderful place has been a greater joy than she could ever have imagined. She says it is fine, and she is ready to go meet her Lord!" Charles shook his head and buried his face in his hands, "But I'm not ready for her to go!" He finished with a moan and dropped his head onto the table.

As Rebecca listened to his words of grief, she felt tears coming to her own eyes. Her heart was aching as she sought for words of comfort to offer.

While his words hung in the air, Rachel stepped forward to take Charles into a motherly embrace. "You will know what to do and say when the time comes," she told him, gently patting him on the back. "You have been living by God's guidance for all these years. He won't desert you now." She continued, "Jennifer and Jean are grown young ladies now, and they have also put their faith in God all through their growing years. All of you will continue to be the strong family your mother and father raised you to be."

Rebecca nodded her head thoughtfully while her mother was talking. *Yes, that is just what I would like to have said. How does she always know just what to say? Does God just give her the right words when she needs them? I pray He will give me that kind of wisdom someday.*

Charles raised his head and looked at his friends through the sheen of unshed tears in his eyes. "Of course, you're right!" he said, "Somehow, I knew that you, my friends, would be able to help me. Our most important job now is to see that her last months or years are the happiest of all of our lives!"

And that was what they did. After the first shock and despair, Jennifer and Jean both proved, as Rachel had said, to be young women strong in their faith in the Lord. The whole family dedicated themselves to making their mother's final years happy. Charles had bought a buggy especially made to give a gentle ride for the occupants. It seemed that no matter how much her health deteriorated, Lucille insisted on being in church. So, each Sunday Charles placed her gently into the buggy, and he would drive carefully, avoiding holes and ruts in the road as they made their way into town. Lucille's face would light with joy as they approached the little church that they had attended faithfully for the years of their time here in the territory. She seemed rejuvenated each time they arrived. She sang joyfully and listened with close attention to everything the ministers said in their sermons. They had had four more pastors since Pastor Farris had been sent to them in 1889. Perhaps a frontier church such as this was hard on a minister, for they were replaced often. Since 1890, Pastors Averyt, Cameron, Patterson, and Worley had all served the church briefly. Lucille would listen raptly to each of the ministers and thank them all sincerely for their sermons. She told her family and close friends constantly how blessed she had been by the pastors' wise advice which applied so well to life in this new territory.

In the year 1891, a cemetery had been built just across the road south from the little community of homes. It was established by the International

Order of Odd Fellows, better known as the IOOF
Lodge. Lucille watched it with interest, and told her
family, "That is where you must bury me! I will lie
there into eternity close to the place and the people I
love." Charles promised that he and the girls would
follow her wishes, but they secretly prayed that they
could postpone that time for many years yet.

In early March of 1893, Lucille quietly drew
her last breath and was laid to rest, just as she had
asked, in the cemetery across the street from her
home of the last four years.

**\*\*\*\***

During Lucille's long illness, it had become
common for Rebecca to spend much time at the
Cunningham's home helping and comforting in any
way she could. A Sunday afternoon soon after the
funeral found her there visiting with the girls.
Charles sat in his easy chair in the living room,
reading his Bible, while Rebecca, Jennifer, and Jean
sat around the kitchen table talking quietly while
drinking tea and eating cookies.

Jean looked around the kitchen and said,
"The food that everybody brought was all so good,
but, now, even with all the people who snacked
when they came for visitation and condolences, there
is still too much left."

Jennifer added, "I wish there were some way
to keep it for later."

"Maybe," said Rebecca thoughtfully, "Maybe
my mother could help. She knows what it is safe to

keep and how long, and what should be used up or thrown away now."

"Do you think she might help?" asked Jennifer.

"Of course, you know she will," said Rebecca, smiling.

Jean drew a long sigh, reached out to her sister and said, "Well, I guess we are on our own. We have a lot to learn. Mom couldn't get up and help with the household, but she was always there for advice."

Jennifer and Jean exchanged a long look and Jennifer said softly, "I guess it's like we promised ourselves, we will be here to take care of Charles as long as he needs us. He will need good meals and a restful home after his hard work on the farm."

"Yes," they both agreed quietly.

In the living room, Charles had suddenly looked up when he heard his name and started to listen carefully. He gently closed his Bible and walked softly into the kitchen.

Rebecca was startled to see him approaching. She looked up at the other girls who had their backs to him. "Oh! It's Charles." She looked nervously from Jennifer to Jean and back to Charles. "Would-- would you like to have a cookie and tea with us?"

"I think I've had enough cookies to last a long time. But now, what is this you girls are planning? Did I understand someone saying that you need to arrange your lives around taking care of me?" Charles looked at all the girls sternly.

"Well," said Jean shakily, "We have been

taking care of the meals and house while mother was so sick and of course we will continue."

Jennifer joined in, "We just figure that you still need someone to take care of the home and garden and all those things. A man living alone can't tend a farm without someone to take care of the household chores."

Charles stood looking at them with a look of understanding beginning to show in his face. "Are you telling me that you girls are planning to spend your lives as spinsters here taking care of me?" When they nodded, he continued. "There are lots of single men living alone in this town and this territory and taking care of themselves! Everything might not be as nice as here when you do it, but I can take care of things!"

Seeing the looks of confusion on his sisters' faces, he continued gently, "I surely wouldn't rush you girls out of our home by any means! But I have wondered why you never seemed to show any interest in any of the young men around. Is this why?"

The girls looked at each other with surprised expressions and nodded silently as Charles continued, "So let's have an understanding. I love you both dearly and want you with me as long as you want to be here, but you are both to live a normal life for young women. And that includes getting to know some men and maybe even finding some nice beaus."

Tearful hugs were exchanged and promises made to do just as Charles had said.

Later, at home, Rebecca pondered over the new relationship that the months just passed had brought about between herself and the whole Cunningham family. She had become like a member of their family as, together, they went through that most difficult time. After taking part in the recent scene with Charles and his sisters, Rebecca worried that she might be intruding on their family privacy. One day when she and Rachel were cleaning up after lunch, she asked her mother about what had developed.

With her hands still in the dishwater, Rachel just shook her head smiling gently, "God knew His plans when He put us all right here in this place together. You are following His leading and being a great comfort to the whole family. They consider you family, and would not discuss any secrets around you that they didn't want you to know."

The families grew ever closer as time went on and the busy community around them demanded their time and attention, leaving them no time to dwell on their grief.

****

Many of the friends they had met during the opening of the territory now had flourishing families in their new homes. The Carpenters, who had opened their general store in town, now had two sweet little girls. Rachel was three years old, and Sally was a pudgy infant. The Bridges who had brought their infant daughter, Mary Annette, with them when they entered the territory, now had, in addition, a busy little two-year-old, Robert Junior. The McFarlin family, faithful members of their church who had come to Norman in 1891 with their daughter Leta, now had a new baby boy whom they had named Robert Boger.

Rebecca looked forward to each Sunday when she helped out with the children during church services. She loved to snuggle the babies and play games with the toddlers. The other friends they had met on the land opening day did not all go to the south church, but the families still saw each other often and rejoiced together when the Millers' two children, Mary Sue and John William were born. The Harrises' livery stable was still flourishing and their family was growing. Martha was now two years old, and Jarrod was a growing infant, who was eager to get down to explore on his own hands and knees.

A heartbreaking time for the community was in 1893 when the McFarlin's baby, Robert, was hit unexpectedly by typhoid fever. The news brought sorrow and fear to people in the town. Small children in frontier areas were often susceptible to food and water-borne diseases. Fortunately, children usually recovered quickly from most of them. However, the word "typhoid" struck fear into the hearts of families of those affected. About all they could do was to fight the fever with cool baths and to wrap them in wet cloths. The doctors always advised the parents to feed them soft foods and broth.

When baby Robert was stricken, his frantic family were doing all that the doctor had told them to do. The friends from the church were praying fervently for his healing. Too soon, though, the word came that in spite of all they could do, young Robert had succumbed to the disease at the very young age of just one year, seven months, and ten days.

Rebecca had become so close to all the children she helped care for on Sunday mornings that the loss was very personal to her. When the day for the funeral arrived, the little church was filled with friends who had come to comfort the McFarlins in their mourning.

The procession from the church to the cemetery seemed endless, and buggies and wagons had to park along every lane and road nearby so the occupants could walk to the tiny grave where the small coffin awaited placement in the ground. Pastor Patterson delivered his final words, and more hugs of comfort and solace were offered. In the quiet that followed, people went silently back to their vehicles and made their sad journeys home.

Not long after the funeral, a simple stone was placed to mark the grave. Rebecca could see the site from the Simpson's home across the road. She visited it often, brushed the dirt from it and cried a few tears. She was intrigued by the small cedar seedling that had come up close-by and fell into the habit of clearing away the weeds and taking a bit of water to it.

The Simpsons, along with many others in the congregation, continued to be concerned for the McFarlin family. They were struggling valiantly to overcome their grief, knowing that their lives had to go on. They tried to console themselves with long days of hard work from dawn to dark. Mr. McFarlin worked untiringly with his herd of cattle, but, still, they did not flourish in the ongoing heat and drought.

After returning from church on a beautiful fall Sunday in October, Rebecca brought up the subject with her family as they sat down for lunch.

"I do so wish that we could find some way to help the McFarlins," she said with tears in her voice. "I can't imagine what it would be like to have lost a sweet baby of my own, but it just breaks my heart to see them carrying around such sorrow week after week. Little Leta doesn't understand at all. This morning she asked me if I could help her find a new baby for her parents so they could be happy again. I thought I would break down and cry right there in the nursery while I was responsible for all those other babies."

"I have felt the same way," said Rachel shaking her head. "I guess everybody has to live out grief in their own way."

"Robert is a different man since this happened," said Daniel. "He has always been a little restless here. I think his real dream is still to have a large successful ranch with thriving cattle. The last time I was in his feed store, he was saying that somewhere in this territory there must be a place where they would have plenty of rain and good pastures for the cattle. I wonder if his restlessness may be partly just thinking that they could get on with their lives better if they were away from this place where they lost their little son."

"Ida tries so hard!" said Rachel sadly. "She tries to give Leta an extra measure of love and attention to be sure she knows that the unhappiness in the home is not her fault!"

"I guess God will work it out in His time," concluded Daniel.

As the family sat down around the table, they included a special prayer for comfort for the McFarlin family as they also offered thanks for the lunch they were about to receive.

****

During these years the situation caused by the years of drought had become dire for many of the settlers. The government and other organizations became aware of the need to offer help. Some relief became available from the Territorial Relief Board in the form of essential food staples. Wherever people gathered together there were vehement arguments over whether this was the best way, or if a work relief program should be devised whereby people would have to earn their supplies.

In the spring of 1891, many of the settlers had found they did not have the seeds they needed for the next year's planting, nor did they have the money to buy them. The Santa Fe Railroad made the seeds available to the farmers who signed promissory notes which would have to be paid off at the end of the season. While the drought was not completely over, the rains were better that season and most of the loans were repaid on schedule.

The weather, however, was not through testing them yet. The Oklahoma Territory seemed to be home to a unique kind of storm that many of the settlers had never seen before coming to Oklahoma. They were called "tornadoes," although some referred to them as "cyclones." At times the sky would turn frighteningly greenish-black and as the people watched in awe, they might see a long twisting funnel of cloud drop down from the sky and dance across the landscape. The storms raced across the countryside leaving devastation as they passed. Most settlers dug underground cellars that could be used as storage, but more importantly, they could hold the entire family, if needed, while a tornado passed. That was just what happened in April of 1893, when two of these storms combined and roared down on Norman. While working in his cornfield, Daniel saw the clouds begin to boil and rotate off toward the west. He raced around to all his neighbors, warning them of the approaching storm and that they should hurry to their cellars. As it turned out, the storm went mainly to the west of them, roaring toward the other sections of Norman and leaving their area untouched. As soon as the danger had passed, and they emerged from their cellars, the men from the undamaged areas raced to the parts of town where the most damage had occurred. It took days of rescue work to assess the complete truth of what had happened. Thirty-one funerals were held in the town as a result of this one storm. Those persons who had observed it approaching or helped in the clean-up afterward said it was a thing that nightmares are made of.

Some of the settlers packed up their goods and their families and left saying that they could not live in a place that could spawn such monstrous storms. For weeks, the neighbors living across from the cemetery observed funerals day after day for those who had been killed.

When the Simpson and Cunningham families discussed it, they agreed that they were fortunate to have survived, but that they had no thoughts of leaving.

"God knows when it is your time," said Daniel, "And it is going to be the same no matter where we are."

Through good times and bad, the tough settlers had held on with faith and determination to the homes and farms they had built on these unbroken lands of the Oklahoma Territory. It had now become their home in the most complete sense of the word. They and their community were growing up together and had become true Oklahomans.

# Chapter 19

## Forward with Joy

*Hello Dear Emmaline,*

*As 1895 begins, I feel a spirit of anticipation that this year will bring great things to us here in Oklahoma Territory. I will observe my nineteenth*

*birthday this year! Even more
unbelievable, my two dear friends,
Jennifer and Jean Cunningham, will
both be twenty! Quietly, without
anyone even noticing it, they have
each found a beau! Jennifer has been
very quietly getting acquainted with
George Williams, a friend we had met
while going to the Wesleyan School
before it became High-Gate College.
He is very handsome. He is the son of
a family who also came in at the run
and claimed land to the west of town. I
have been noticing the special looks
they exchange each Sunday at church,
and the last time we had a church
dinner, they quietly took their plates to
a table together!*

*For several Sundays lately,
Jean has asked permission to go
across to the services at the North
Methodist church! When I teased her
to know what she was doing, she
admitted that she was going to
services with Jonathan Morton and his
family. She even admitted that they
were beginning to talk of marriage!*

*The churches in Norman are
continuing to grow, including ours.
Our minister and trustees are telling
us that something must be done to
have more room for our congregation.*

*It breaks my heart when they discuss tearing down our little building and replacing it with a larger one. Our poor little building that was built around a small house six years ago does not look like much, but has become very dear to me and many others!*

*However, we must* plan for the future! That is the spirit that brought us here to begin with, and now, *God continues to lead us forward...*

The families in the congregation went home either excited or sorrowing that day after the minister had announced the plans to tear down their little building and replace it. The Cunninghams and the Simpsons had gathered for lunch around the Cunninghams' table. Even though it had been over a year now since Lucille's death, the house still seemed empty without her there. Jennifer and Jean had left a roast and vegetables cooking slowly in the oven while they went to church and now, they had spread the meal on the table before the two families.

"It makes me so sad to think that our cozy little church will be gone," began Rebecca mournfully. "It is the only church we have known for six years now. It just won't seem right to worship somewhere else!"

"But just think," said Jean with her eyes shining. "A larger building, more rooms for classes, and a sanctuary large enough to have a piano."

"I must admit that I am looking forward to all those things," said Rachel thoughtfully. "But I have come to love that funny looking little building too. I don't think I can bear to go see it when it is being torn down!"

Daniel considered for a few moments then put in, "It is true that that little building has served its purpose well and we all love it, but we are forward-looking people. We wouldn't be here in this territory if we weren't. I believe Pastor Sherwood is right when he says that if our congregation is to continue to grow, we must have room to grow in."

"Well, the announcement did one thing that no one would have expected," said Jennifer with a hesitant smile and her cheeks showing a faint blush.

As everybody turned to look at her, she continued, "George asked me right after the service if I would mind if he comes to ask Charles for permission to ask for my hand!"

With looks of amazement from the whole group and squeals from the other two girls, Jennifer continued, "Of course I told him that I would certainly be happy for him to come see you, Charles."

Charles grinned, shaking his head slowly, "I guess it was bound to happen sometime, but somehow this doesn't seem to make much sense. He asked Jennifer for permission to see me to ask me for permission to marry her." He spread his hands in a comical gesture of total puzzlement.

Jennifer turned her brightest smile on her brother, "Of course it makes sense. He had to know whether I was likely to answer 'yes' before he got your permission. We had been talking about it for a while, but now starting to build a new church changes things. We both love our little church, and we want to be married there before it is torn down." She turned back to her brother to say, "He is coming by this afternoon at about three o'clock." Then she added innocently, "Is that okay?"

"I wonder what everybody at this table would do to me if I said it wasn't okay, or that I was too busy?" asked Charles with a teasing smile.

Daniel scratched his jaw thinking, "I talked to the pastor for a little while after the service, and he thinks the demolition will happen very soon. Maybe within a couple of months." He raised his eyebrows as he looked toward Rachel.

Rachel understood his unspoken question and told the whole group. "If Charles gives permission for George to ask for her hand, and Jennifer says yes to the proposal, you can count on the Simpson family to do everything possible to help you have a beautiful wedding in our dear little church."

After the kitchen was cleaned up, the Simpsons returned to their own home, and, just a little before 3:00, a buggy pulled up at the Cunninghams. George Williams got out still dressed in his Sunday suit and went up on the porch to knock at the door.

The Simpson family couldn't resist the urge to peer out their windows curiously as the time passed while George was inside next door. After about an hour, George and the entire Cunningham family came out on the porch. Jennifer and George were holding hands. Charles was laughing and joking with George as the two clapped each other on the shoulders. After a time, George climbed back into the buggy and drove off as the others waved.

As soon as he was out of sight, Jennifer and Jean ran to the Simpsons' house and were met on the porch by the family.

"It's 'yes'," squealed Jean excitedly, "I am going to be maid-of-honor for Jennifer's wedding!"

Daniel chuckled, "So, I guess this means that Charles said 'yes' he could ask Jennifer, and she said 'yes' she would marry him?"

"Of course, I knew all along what I would say. George says he has already asked Pastor Sherwood when the building will be coming down," said Jennifer. "He said about two months so they can get started building on the new one when spring comes."

Rachel studied Jennifer carefully, "Well, I think two months is plenty of time to make a very nice wedding gown. We might even manage to make some dresses for bridesmaids too." She paused to look teasingly at Jennifer, "That is, just as long as you don't recruit every girl in the church."

"Oh! Thank you so much! I don't sew well enough to make anything myself." Jennifer hurried across the room to give Rachel a hug. "I don't want anyone else besides Jean as maid-of-honor, and Rebecca as bridesmaid."

Rachel returned the hug and said, "I think I can manage three dresses in two months. We must go to town tomorrow to get fabric and patterns."

So it was that, early the next morning, Rachel and three excited young women headed into Norman to search for the perfect fabrics and patterns for the bride and wedding party. It was several hours later when the happy group returned. Eager to show their purchases, they called the men in and held the filmy, soft fabrics up to themselves while sharing the plans they had made.

The bride would wear a beautiful white embroidered silk made very simply with a fitted bodice and long, flared skirt. Jean would wear the same style in the same silk fabric only in a sky blue. Rebecca's dress would match the other two in soft rose pink.

The three girls held their fabrics up to themselves and made a solemn parade as if marching down the aisle. Watching them, Rachel, Daniel, and Charles clapped and began to sing, "Here comes the bride."

"I have an idea. I know what we can do," Jean stopped the solemn march. "Jennifer, Rebecca, and I can share all the housework and cooking for both houses, so Rachel can spend all her time sewing!"

"Yes, yes!" chimed in the other girls.

"I just can't wait to see my dress," said Rebecca nuzzling her face gently into the soft pink fabric.

Rachel smiled at the three excited young women, "Now that sounds like a deal I can't refuse."

"Can we help you cut them right now?"

asked the bride-to-be.

So, the women cleared off the dining room table and soon the three were pinning and measuring.

"This fabric is so beautiful, I am almost afraid to cut into it," Rachel mused as she held the scissors hesitantly above it.

"Oh, Mother, you know there is no one who sews like you do," said Rebecca encouragingly. "You know it will turn out beautifully."

By the time Jennifer and Jean returned to their own home, three dresses had been cut out and the pieces were stacked neatly on the Simpsons' table ready for the sewing machine tomorrow.

For the next month, Rachel spent most of the daytime hours busily pedaling keeping the machine whirring, and soon three beautiful dresses appeared. While she was sewing, the girls followed through on their promise to keep the houses cleaned and delicious hot meals on the tables.

Daniel kidded Charles, saying, "You can tell George that he is lucky to be marrying a very accomplished housekeeper and cook."

Picking up the spirit of the joke, Charles scratched his head as if puzzled while looking at Jennifer, "I wonder why I never saw any of these talents before?"

"Oh, Charles," said Jennifer, hitting him playfully on the arm, "You know I do those same things at home all the time!"

Serious for a moment, Charles took his sister by the shoulders and pulled her into a hug. "Maybe I shouldn't have given my permission to George. I'm not sure I can give you up."

"What if I decide to get married too," asked Jean mischievously. "Then you would miss us with neither a housekeeper nor cook."

"Well," Charles said softly looking around the room, "I'll just have to give that some thought."

It was surprising how quickly the necessary preparations were completed. The promised cleaning and cooking were done in record time, leaving the girls plenty of time to write out invitations on the beautiful stationery they had bought. The invitations announced the wedding date as Saturday, March 30, 1895. These were delivered to their neighbors and their friends at church.

True to promises, all was in readiness by the chosen date and the happy families gathered in their beloved little church to witness as Jennifer Cunningham and George Williams were pronounced Mr. and Mrs. George Williams by Pastor Sherwood. After all the festivities were over, the couple was sent off to their new home on George's farm on the West side of Norman. It was a subdued group who got into their buggies and headed back to their homes.

Jean was a little teary-eyed. "All the time we were moving Jennifer's things out yesterday, it didn't quite seem real but now it is too real! The house is going to be so empty and quiet. I have never been without my twin before!"

In a short time, the families adjusted to the fact that Jennifer was now a young married woman, and had a home of her own on a small farm on the west side of Norman near George's parents. After being such close neighbors and sharing so much of their lives during recent years, the two families now found themselves together even more. Breakfast was most often the only meal eaten at home while each day included an agreement early in the day about which family would prepare the lunch and which would make the dinner.

As spring came and summer approached, the shared meals were a very practical arrangement. It left the women time to work in the garden and join with their other neighbors for canning and preserving the crops as well as finding time for sewing, reading, or other activities.

As expected, it was not long after Jennifer and George's wedding that the little building was taken down. Many, like Rachel, were greatly saddened and could not bear to go by and see the empty lot. The sense of unity in the congregation continued, and in fact, it increased even more as construction began on the new building at the old location.

They had found a temporary meeting place in a warehouse belonging to the Norman Cotton Oil Mill. All of the familiar furnishings from the old building were moved there, and the congregation happily sang the old familiar songs of praise. Some pointed out that it was still a warehouse and were reminded by Pastor Sherwood that wherever they gathered in His name God would be there.

As the months passed, the congregation flourished in the temporary setting, enjoying fellowship with both new and old members. Many were saddened in the middle of 1895 when Robert McFarlin made known to his friends in both the church and his business that he was making plans to take his cattle business to the eastern part of the territory where the rains were plentiful. Even though the drought around Norman had loosened its grip, Mr. McFarlin felt it was too uncertain to depend on. That year he took his cattle to a leased farm in the small town of Fentriss, which was soon renamed Holdenville. There the cattle did thrive, but it was a lonely existence for Mr. McFarlin as he considered the town too primitive a place to bring his wife and child. He returned to his family and community in Norman regularly while caring for his cattle in Holdenville. He planned to continue the arrangement for as many years as needed until he considered the newer town to be safe.

As they always did, the congregation banded together to help Ida McFarlin in any way they could. She was an independent, self-reliant woman, well able to handle the pioneering life she and Robert had led but she was wise enough to recognize the value of her many church and business friendships. It was also during this period that baby Pauline was born and Ida was showered with offers of help with Leta and the new baby.

****

While these events were taking place, the Simpson and Cunningham families continued to experience life-changing events. One Sunday afternoon late in May of 1895, Jonathan Morton showed up on the Cunninghams' porch dressed in his Sunday best. The events played out much as they had earlier when George had come calling about marrying Jennifer. Permission was soon given, the proposal accepted, and it was then time to plan a wedding for Jonathan and Jean.

Jean and Jonathan set their wedding date for Saturday, September 28, 1895, in the First Methodist Episcopal Church.

Two new dresses were called for since the two girls were so different in height and build that there was no possibility of altering the dresses from Jennifer's wedding to reuse them. It might have been possible to cut down the tall Jennifer's bridal gown, but they all realized that Jennifer might very well have a daughter someday who would want to be married in it. Also, it was obviously impossible for petite Jean's maid-of-honor dress to be made over for a woman as tall as Jennifer. It was decided, however, that they could keep the same style for the new items and Rebecca could still wear her dress from Jennifer's wedding. Since the south church was now being rebuilt, the wedding would take place across the block at the north church where Jonathan's family belonged. Jonathan proudly took the family of his intended over and introduced them to Pastor J. L. Bean, who was delighted for the opportunity to officiate the ceremony in his church.

Again, Rachel spent many enjoyable days at her sewing machine turning out the beautiful new dresses. Just as before, Jean and Rebecca took over all the household chores to free up Rachel's time. The two girls were turning into accomplished homemakers, and life continued smoothly in the two homes while Rachel turned out the finery for the coming festivities.

One evening Jonathan had been invited for the evening meal with the two families at the Simpsons' house. When the meal had been finished, the table was cleared and the dishes were carried into the kitchen, Charles stepped forward to usher Rachel and Daniel into their own living room, along with Jonathan, and Jean.

"Rachel you cooked this wonderful meal, and it is time for you and Daniel to sit down and get to know Jonathan better," he said. "I already know Jonathan well, so Rebecca can wash and I will dry the dishes while you four go talk! Isn't that right Rebecca?"

Rebecca looked at him with an expression akin to amazement. "Do you know how to dry dishes? I don't think I have ever seen you with a dishtowel in your hands!" she said laughingly, "And I know I have never seen you dry a dish!"

Charles grasped her shoulders and urged her toward the kitchen. "All the better for you to teach me! I won't have any bad habits to unlearn!"

While the others regarded them with looks of wonder, the two moved companionably to the kitchen and their task of the evening. When they were at the sink with aprons tied on to protect their clothes, Rebecca washed the first plate, dipped it into hot rinse water, and held it out to him.

"Now," she said, "What is this really about?"

Charles backed off, holding up his hands and protesting innocently, "What do you mean 'What is it about?' I just thought it would be nice to give your mom a rest."

"Hmm!" said Rebecca with raised eyebrows. "We'll see."

As they dropped the banter and just enjoyed working together, the conversation ranged over many subjects. Having lived next door to each other for six years, they were well acquainted enough to be comfortable sharing their thoughts about everything from their beliefs about God to the future of their beloved Oklahoma Territory.

After a while, Rebecca mused, "With all the young unmarried women around and so many of them thinking of marriage," she paused and looked directly at him, "How is it that an eligible twenty-three-year-old man like you has managed to avoid being paired up and keeping company with any of them?"

Charles put down his dish towel and said with all teasing gone from his voice, "Well, many years ago, I saw a beautiful young woman who wore her hair in long braids and had a calico dress with a white apron. It's true there are many beautiful women in Norman, but I have never seen one to equal that one so long ago. I am keeping company right this minute with the only woman I am interested in. I always knew from the first day we met that I would wait for you." Rebecca's mouth dropped open as she turned to him, and he continued, "I guess it is time you should know that before some of those other eligible men start wanting to keep company with you. Which brings up the question, why have you never shown any interest in any of them?"

Rebecca opened her mouth to speak, and shut it again. She raised her hands with dishwater dripping from them and looked at them in wonder as if she could not think what to do with them.

Charles took the towel and carefully dried her hands. "Am I wrong?" he asked softly.

"I....I," she looked away and took a deep breath, "I never thought it was possible. I've never been interested in any men because I always dreamed of growing up and finding someone just like you, so, of course, none of the others ever seemed to measure up. I once told your sisters that I was waiting for someone who saw me like a fine lady, and would be my noble knight. I always remembered those times when we first came here when you bowed and called me "My Lady." But I was sure that I was too young and you must be just teasing. You couldn't possibly have been interested in me!"

"Yes, when I first knew you, you were young, but I could see that inside that girl was the woman you are now. I could see her even then and knew that I would wait as long as needed until you and your parents considered you ready to be keeping company with me." Charles, now, was completely serious as he reached for her hand. "May I ask your father for permission to court you?'

"I think," said Rebecca shakily, "I think that would make me very happy."

It was a magic moment as the two looked into each other's eyes. Just as Charles slipped his arm around Rebecca's waist, Rachel appeared in the door saying, "It is taking an awfully long time to get those dishes done. Charles must need a lot of teaching in the art of dish drying!"

As soon as she saw the expressions of the two, she continued with a smile, "Oh, is that it? It is not the art of doing dishes that is occupying your attention."

"No, Mama," said Rebecca wonderingly, "I can't believe it!"

"I can," said Rachel taking Rebecca in her arms. "I have known it for years, probably almost as long as Charles has."

"Maybe we better go in the living room," said Charles. "I need to get Daniel's permission to court the most wonderful young woman in the whole Oklahoma Territory!"

With that, the relationship changed subtly. They were no longer an adult neighbor and the girl next door. They were now officially a courting couple, and it seemed obvious to all that it was just a matter of time before courting led to an engagement.

The days settled into a routine through the summer as the preparations for Jonathan and Jean moved along easily to be ready for that September date. Finally, with the heat of summer past, the weather became pleasantly cool as the season turned to autumn. September 28 arrived, and families and friends gathered in the First Methodist Episcopal Church to celebrate the union of Jean Cunningham and Jonathan Morton.

As Charles escorted his sister to the altar, his eyes went to Rebecca standing there as a bridesmaid. Jean was exquisite in her bridal gown, and Jennifer was a radiant matron of honor. Charles, though, had eyes only for Rebecca. They exchanged a look and an agreement passed between them that it would not be long before they were the wedding couple.

After Charles had completed all his brotherly duties at the reception, he took Rebecca's hand and pulled her outside into the beautiful autumn afternoon.

"I talked to Pastor Sherwood earlier today," he told her. "I asked him when they expect to be in the new building."

"Oh!" Rebecca replied eagerly, "Does he know, or maybe have an estimated date?"

"He says we are almost sure to be in by December 1897." Charles ducked his head holding his chin with thumb and forefinger. He looked at her from the corners of his eyes, "I wondered if we could maybe be the first couple married in the new building."

Rebecca clapped her hands and closed her eyes for a moment as if seeing events playing in her mind. "Wouldn't that be wonderful? A winter wedding could be so beautiful! That's over a year away right now. We might wait until the time is closer next year before we set the date, and maybe they will have a closer estimate."

"I think if I tell Pastor Sherwood what we have in mind, he would probably keep us informed as they get more information so we could know when to set the date." agreed Charles.

"Won't it be fun to have the first wedding in the new building?" said Rebecca, with her enthusiasm growing. "Just wait till I tell Mama!"

Having agreed upon this plan, they hurried to tell their families and friends, and they settled into a life full of anticipation and preparation.

Soon after 1897 dawned and was underway the community was saddened by the news from the McFarlin family that they would be moving to Holdenville soon. Robert had been missing his family greatly, and he had decided that the town had now matured enough to move his family there.

In telling their friends of their plans, Robert said, "You can be sure you will be seeing us often. A part of our hearts is out there in the cemetery. In time, when our financial situation is improved, there will be a monument out there in addition to the marker. It will be a monument to turn that space into a garden for a young child."

The family had made for themselves a lasting place in the hearts and minds of the community. So, it was, with a sense of loss, that the town and congregation expressed their best wishes. Pastor Sherwood phrased it well for the whole community, when he said, "We will just say 'Until we meet again' because you have put your imprint on this community and we know we will be hearing from you again."

****

There were many things to be done and many plans to make as the families looked ahead to another wedding. As the year went along, they received frequent reports from Pastor Sherwood on the status of the construction. When they went to visit the building site, the progress was obvious. They were able to wander through the rooms and visualize where the altar was to be and where all the members of the wedding party would be placed. They could also see the fellowship room where they would hold a reception afterward. Rebecca even visualized the flowers and decorations they would use to carry out the color theme of the women's dresses.

Since it appeared that it would be a winter wedding, Rebecca asked Jean and Jennifer if they didn't think that maybe they should use some more winterish fabrics than the light silks they had used for the other two weddings. They all agreed and went shopping to see what was available.

Their friends, the Carpenters had, some time ago, expanded their store and put in a fabric section that was the largest in Norman. What they didn't have in the store, they could order and have delivered within the month. The three girls arrived and went straight to Charlotte to get her opinion about what fabrics to use.

Of course, since the two families were good

friends, they first visited with the Carpenters' two children for a while. Amanda, who was now seven years old, was deep into reading a book, *Alice in Wonderland,* by Lewis Carroll. She was pleased at the chance to explain the story to the three visitors.

Sally waited patiently for her turn to tell their friends about her new stuffed bear. After it was properly admired, the trio finally got down to their shopping.

Rebecca began by explaining to Charlotte what they were looking for. "You see, we want some sort of heavier materials than the filmy silk we had for Jennifer and Jean's weddings. Sky blue and rose pink are still our favorite colors though."

Charlotte put her finger to her cheek and looked around the store thoughtfully. "Here is something that is new. It is all cotton, but with a very tight weave. It comes out with a nice sheen and then can be decorated with designs. I only have a few colors in the store, but since it is only April, I am sure we could get any color you want in time to get the dresses made."

The three friends felt the soft, firm material and nodded to each other. "Oh yes," said Jennifer. "This is so nice and soft. Just look at this blue one, I love the way it has a slightly deeper shade of blue over it."

"Here it is in pink, too!" exclaimed Jean, "and with the same two shades effect! I can just see my dress made of this!"

"Believe it or not, I would not have thought that there were shades of white," explained

Charlotte, "But there is actually a two-tone white in the same fabric."

"I think these are just what we need!" said Rebecca, putting the fabric up to her cheek to feel how smooth it was. "I think we should plan to use the same pattern we used for your weddings," Rebecca looked at her two friends as she spoke. "If we want to, we can have Mama add some longer sleeves to them."

"That is a wonderful idea! I can't believe we have already found just what we wanted! And now we won't even have to order and wait for it." said Jean, turning to Charlotte.

"I can hardly wait to get home and have Rachel start on them." added Jennifer.

Rebecca put her arms around her two friends, "Won't she be proud of us for making up our minds so quickly." She took a look at the price tag on the fabric with a look of surprise. "Not only that, but we have also chosen a very inexpensive fabric. This is not nearly as expensive as the silk we used before."

For the next two months, the machine whirred busily again as Rachel produced more gowns that were indeed works of art! They were all hanging, covered by sheets, inside the closet just awaiting the word for when the big day would be.

It seemed like a long wait until September when Pastor Sherwood gave them the report that the building was promised to be ready by the middle of November. The wedding party visited the nearly complete building and marveled at the beautiful fixtures and woodwork that were now completed.

They were now ready to set the wedding date and get down to final plans. The dedication of the building was planned for November 21, so they set the wedding date for Saturday, November 27.

When the day finally arrived, the church was filled to overflowing. These two families had been in town since the very beginning of settlement here and had made many friends who wanted to be there to see them step into their new life together. It seemed that the whole town was there packed into the beautiful new sanctuary.

Rachel watched with love and joy as the wedding party came slowly down the aisle to the music from the shiny, new upright piano. Charles and the pastor entered to stand in front of the altar; the two young matrons-of-honor floated down the aisle on the arms of their husbands. Their shades of rose pink and sky blue brought an air of spring to the sanctuary which was kept cozily warm by the large new pot-bellied stove.

Finally, Daniel gave the radiant Rebecca his arm and escorted her down the aisle to wed the man that he already cherished like a son. The ceremonies were brief but beautiful, and it seemed like no time at all until it was over.

Rebecca and Charles turned to face the congregation as Pastor Sherwood said, "I present to you, Mr. and Mrs. Charles Cunningham."

The happy couple walked down the aisle and led the way to the fellowship room for their reception. A joyous hour was spent greeting and being greeted by their many friends.

When the last guest had departed, they headed toward the front door of the beautiful new church. They looked at each other with a nod and a smile as they stepped through the door with a feeling of assurance that this event was a momentous one. Only God could know what awaited them in the years ahead, but they looked forward with joy!

# Epilogue

Melissa Conroy closed the first book from the chest. She was surprised to find that she had been reading through the night.

She hugged it closely to herself, as she breathed a prayer, "Thank you God for the chance to meet some of my ancestors and those who have gone with them in this place and this church. I am so honored to have the opportunity to continue this task."

Looking at the hour, she saw that it was too early to go to her mother yet, so she snuggled into her covers for a while thinking about the stories she had read. She was awakened from a light sleep after an hour had passed, and she could hear her mother in the kitchen preparing breakfast.

She quickly got out of bed, put on her robe, and hurried to the kitchen to embrace her mother. "Of course, I want to do it! Did you really have any doubts whether I would want the privilege of being the one to continue recording this wonderful story?"

"I was hoping this was the way you would feel," her mother said smiling. "That is just the way I felt when the chest was given to me. This story will not be over for a long time yet. God still has much in store for this family, and this McFarlin congregation."

Melissa hurried back to her room and sat down to look again through the stack of journals she had read through the night. Some of them looked almost new, while others were yellow and brown with age. She looked at the most recent one that included her mother's writings with the last entry made just yesterday. Her mother had written:

> *Hello, dear Emmaline,*
>
> *My heart is heavy as I consider passing the responsibility of writing your letters. I loved having the opportunity to be the person to carry on this tradition, but I fear that*

*I have not been very faithful. I have only made a few entries during my years as your correspondent. Writing has become so difficult for me. The doctor says my crippled, painful hands are due to severe arthritis. Wouldn't you think that with the advanced stages of medicine we have now that they would have found a cure? But they haven't, and I fear that many of my writings have been rather incomplete.*

*I think that Melissa will be pleased to receive this gift on her eighteenth birthday tomorrow. Since she has always loved stories of both our family and our church history, I think she will be delighted to take this job. I will be very surprised if she is not! So, after tomorrow, I expect that you will be meeting your new correspondent.*

*I pray it will be as much a blessing to her as it has been to me!*
*Your dear friend,*
*Janelle Conroy*

With a hint of tears in her eyes, Melissa picked up the quaint little fountain pen that had been in the box all those years since it was first given to Rebecca Simpson Cunningham. Noting that it still had ink from her mother's last writing, she opened the journal to a new page and caressed the fine paper lovingly. At the top of the page, adding a little extra flourish, she wrote in her finest handwriting:

> *Hello Dear Emmaline,*
> *My name is Melissa Conroy,*
> *and I am sure we are going to be the*
> *best of friends! . . .*

# About the Author

I was born in Norman, Oklahoma in 1937. In 1956, Joe Sanders and I were married at McFarlin United Methodist Church in Norman. The next 20 years were spent and enjoyed in the places where Joe's career in the US Marine Corps took us. Norman and central Oklahoma have been the "return-to" places for myself and our children when Joe had tours where we could not accompany him. We returned to the area in 1976 upon Joe's retirement from the USMC. Today we live in Norman, and are faithful members of McFarlin UMC.

I am a retired Middle School Math teacher with a love for reading and writing. I discovered a love and fascination for the unique history of McFarlin United Methodist Church while on a committee for planning the 75th anniversary celebration for the church. At that time, I wrote *With God's Help; Building the McFarlin Church* and *This in Our Church*, two historical fiction books for young adults and children. My writings also include several unpublished works, which are home-printed books for the information and entertainment of family, children, and grandchildren. Our family favorite of these is *The Amazing Adventures of Whiteboots,* which was written about our family cat who lived with us for over fifteen truly amazing years.

    At this time, I am feeling a compulsion to tell more of the stories of the fictional characters and their families from *With God's Help*. This current book is the first installment in those planned works. At this point in the writing, however, the name, Cunningham is the only thing you would recognize from that book.

# A Word from the Author

Thank you for reading this book. I hope that you have enjoyed meeting these fictional families along with some of the real people who have been so important in McFarlin's history. I hope you have not been distracted by my imperfect attempts at drawings. During this writing, visions of these people and events have paraded through my head constantly until I felt compelled to make this effort to share them with you through my own drawings.

It is my plan to continue their stories in *Into a World of Madness,* Part two of *Journey in Faith.* In part two, our friends and their church will cope with the nation's involvement in World War. They will rejoice in the building of a new church near the OU campus, and experience the reuniting of the North and South branches of Methodism.

It is my earnest prayer that I will be able to complete the next installment as planned.

# Sources of Information

This book is a work of historical fiction. The Robert McFarlin family, the ministers of the churches, and other public figures were real people. They and the events surrounding them have been kept as true to historical events as available knowledge allows.

The families portrayed in relation to the events of 1889 and the following years are fictional. I believe, however, that there were families like these in the many towns that popped up overnight all over the Unassigned Lands. They must all have coped with the same or similar problems and dealt with similar failures and rewards. The information to make these people as close as possible to the kind of people who lived these events has been found in a variety of sources that must be recognized.

The Oklahoma Territorial Museum in Guthrie, Oklahoma, contains a wealth of information dramatically presented in dioramas which cover exactly the everyday facts of making a life on the Oklahoma frontier that I needed for this work. Michael Williams at that Museum in Guthrie, was extremely patient and helpful throughout my work. He promptly and completely answered my dozens of emailed questions about inconsequential details of life during the time after the run.

The cover photo for this book comes from

many different sources in the McFarlin United Methodist Church Archives. Two of these are *Golden Anniversary 1924-1974,* and *A Priceless Heritage: Shining Diamond Bright for 75 Years*, Both of these are written by Mary Joyce Rodgers.

**The following published works have been especially helpful:**

Belknap, Lucille S. *Beginnings, Oklahoma, Norman, The Little Church.* Transcript Press, Norman, Oklahoma. 1980,

Hoig, Stan. *The Oklahoma Land Rush of 1889.* Oklahoma Historical Society. 1984.

Rodgers, Mary Joyce. *A Priceless Heritage: Shining Diamond Bright for 75 Years*, McFarlin United Methodist Church. Norman, Oklahoma. 1999.

Rodgers, Mary Joyce. *Golden Anniversary 1924-1974*, McFarlin United Methodist Church, Norman, Oklahoma. Hooper Printing Co., Inc. 1974.

Speer, Bonnie. *Cleveland County, Pride of the Promised Land.* Traditional Publishers, Norman, OK. 1988,

Womack, John. Norman---*An Early History. 1820-1990.* 1976.